Other Books by Linda J Pifer

Ohio Girl – a Memoir

Windows
Book One in the Windows Trilogy

Daniel Smith
New Zealand Passage – Book Two

Copper Swift
Return to High Bridge – Book Three

Visit the author's website at:
http://www.lindajpiferauthor.com

THISTLE & STONE

BY LINDA J PIFER

Cover design by Linda J Pifer

Cover Photography by Pond5

Published by Readingseat Books
An LLC Company – U.S.

Available from Amazon.com and other book stores.

ISBN: 978-0-9890142-6-7

First Edition

As always –

To the ones I love; the most patient family ever as I sit at the computer somewhere in cyberspace... so wonderful to have your love and understanding.

And to Roselyn who at 91 is still writing and sets an example for us all.

Linda

(The wife, 'mudder', and grandma)

Table of Contents

Within seconds the room began to whirl in a flash of neon-blue light and she grabbed the nearest lions-head ring with both hands as the floor fell away from her feet.

CHAPTER One – Vacation

The menagerie of reclaimed treasures enticed and caught an avid customer; Shelley Lindquist parked and locked her car in front of the salvage company just outside of Atlanta. Her mother always said she was drawn 'like a bear to honey' to this stuff and Shelley acknowledged it; a decorator by trade, she made the place part of her first mini-vacation in ten years.

The warehouse was surrounded by a clutter of reclamation treasures. At a glance Shelley could discern several twelve-paned windows with peeling paint leaning against a wall. Spear-like lightning rods from old barns were stuffed into a wooden barrel, their decorative tips pointed upward as if ready to launch. On the other side of the door, three claw-foot tubs sat end to end strangely impressive as they waited for their next clients to bath, with pedestal sinks nearby.

Her boys, Mark and Jason, stayed home with their grandmother for the week and she felt some guilt though it was her first time away since their birth ten years ago. When Mark Sr. left to chase a career in Hong Kong, it became the three of them against the world and a divorce followed. This vacation had flown, but she'd spent none of it rehashing regrets over her worthless ex-husband.

A stack of rusty ceiling tiles beside the door caused her to stop and admire their hard- to- duplicate layers of peeling paint and weathered finish. An old bronze garden statue of a hound dog sat nearby and she drifted into 'how to use him' mode for a decorating scheme and took a picture; her clients loved this stuff.

Inside the warehouse, high rafters displayed stained-glass panels hung against the natural light from windows behind; their multiple colors of deep blue, purple, red and yellow cast over everything below. It was the biggest open collection of repurposed items she'd ever seen and it took a few moments to fight child-like excitement and choose an aisle to begin exploring.

"Something tells me one day isn't enough here, this is my nirvana." She whispered.

Hours later, Shelley found a large room with every style entry door she could imagine; timber and wood, battened and ledged, framed and paneled were displayed row on row, many complete with the original glass lights and frames. She was side-tracked before entering and stopped to examine a shabby-chic table outside the door.

"Quite the collection here, eh?" An older gentleman said from a nearby Victorian chair.

"My goodness, where did you come from?" Shelley said, surprised at his voice because she'd failed to see him before as she passed by.

"From here and thare." He said. "Guess ye didna see me."

"I didn't, do you work here?"

"Gae on inside." He invited and ignored her question. "Tak yer time, there's routh ta see."

"Thank you, it's a wonderful array. How old are some of these pieces?"

"Older than ye'd think fer this part o' the world, many oreeginal to Europe an brocht over." He got to his feet and searched her face. "Are ye interestit in architecture? Most are curiosity seekers hereaboots."

She stepped back to regain her personal space. "My father was a heritage architect. He always had books and vintage blueprints strewn about the house before he passed; he's why I'm an interior designer. I've been familiar with periods of design from an early age."

"That so? Then ye might apprise two older pieces in here." Shelley hung on his words to understand him through his heavy Scots accent. He motioned to the open room. "In fact, I'd be pleased ta shaw them ta ye."

He led the way with a visible limp, but kept up a good pace. Shelley took in his worn clothing and graying, shaggy hair as she followed and decided he looked as venerable as the items in the warehouse.

"Jest ta your left here." He turned to another aisle that wound through more displays. High windows let in the afternoon sun through dusty panes, and beveled glass in several doors caught the late afternoon beams.

"Ah, here we are." He said over his shoulder, but she noticed a pair of European-style doors along the way and stopped to admire them.

"These are lovely." She reached to touch their verdigris, hammered copper, but he returned and took her wrist. "What are you doing?" She said as he led her a few rows further then released her.

Her temper flared, but she forgot his rudeness when she saw the huge pair of dark wooden doors towering over her. At least twelve feet high, their tops almost touched the room's ceiling.

"They're magnificent; from the medieval period aren't they and heavy enough to defend any fortress; where are they from?" She heard no reply and turned to repeat the question, but the old man was gone.

After a glance up and down the aisle, she forgot him and returned to the giant doors. A large, iron lion-head with a heavy ring in his mouth was centered on each door and she couldn't help thinking how excited her father would be over them.

She reached to rest her hand on the cool iron of one lion's head and a blue static charge flew to her fingers. Laughing, she took her hand away and thought the static charge unusual for this time of year.

Within seconds the whole room began to whirl in a flash of neon-blue light. She grabbed the nearest lions-head ring with both hands and felt the floor fall away from her feet.

She clung to the door, helpless to control what was happening as it began to spin, slowly at first then increasingly faster.

Her perception of time and place began to fade and thoughts of escape drifted away as she stared with strange calm into the fantastic, starry space before her.

CHAPTER Two - Reality

Shelley awoke on a hard grey-stone floor and leaned against the doors from the warehouse, the only objects she recognized. Two grey-stone stairways wound to a second level on either side of the cavernous room; a massive fireplace blazed far away at its opposite end.

"Where am I?" Her voice echoed without response. Shaky and uncertain, she stood and braced against the door's solidness before taking a step forward. The vaulted ceiling appeared at least twenty feet high, the floor underfoot was cold through her sandals; in fact, the room was freezing so she decided to walk toward the fireplace until she could think through what had just happened.

There were banners hung high along the walls, shields and archaic weapons displayed between them. She rubbed a hand over the stone wall; someone invested time and expense here, the decorator in her observed. It can't be a theme park, there's no plastic or fiberglass; the owner must be deep into the 14th Century.

A niggling thought arose; is this real? Her practical response was 'get a grip and don't be ridiculous Shelley'. Thus self-coached, she continued through the room and tried to figure out her surroundings.

As she came nearer the fireplace she realized a large dog was lying on the hearth staring at her. Of course, she thought, what else do I need but a gigantic, Irish wolfhound? Remembering what her father taught her about strange dogs, she held her hands out, palms down and stood still. The animal arose and began its slow pace toward her, sniffing out her scent. Without warning, the dog broke into a trot then stopped short as she put up her arms and prepared to be eaten. Instead, he reached to lob several slobbery kisses across her face.

"Oh good grief. Okay boy, okay." Her attempts to push the large creature back didn't work and their combined weight landed them both on a small sheepskin rug.

"Oof!" Her breath escaped her, but she was okay and suppressed a giggle. She tried again to repel the friendly hound who just wanted to play. Finally he quieted and laid his head on her chest to stare into her eyes. "Ok boy, I have to get up!" She wiggled out from under the devoted hound and stood.

After wiping her face on her sleeve, she noticed a man watching her who was strangely similar to the older man in the warehouse. He looked different though, younger somehow, his hair a dark brown instead of gray and with no lines on his face. How could that be? Perhaps he is the old man's son; confusion reigned.

"What is this place and how did I get here?" She said.

"A good question; now I'll ask some." He walked towards her. "How did you get inside?" He stopped in front of her; the dog looked from one to the other and sent a sharp bark echoing off the Hall.

"Jakke!" the man commanded him by name. "Down!" He waved a hand to the floor and Jakke obeyed with a whine.

"Perhaps we should sit over here to appear less threatening to... Jakke, is it?" Shelley started to move to one of the benches along the wall.

"Where do you think you're going?" He grabbed her arm. "You can't enter uninvited and proceed to make yourself comfortable. Who are you and what do you want?"

"You know more than me, you were at the warehouse. And stop grabbing my arm, it isn't polite, in case you haven't heard." She twisted out of his hold. "Why don't <u>you</u> start with why I'm here?"

Something in her fearlessness and the way she stood her ground made him think twice about how he'd move forward. "Well, you're not like the rest; perhaps this time..." His thoughts drifted toward a new method for handling the intruder.

"AGNES." He bellowed. A middle-aged woman came from a doorway next to the fireplace, casting a quick look at the stranger as she passed by. "Yes sir?"

"Food and drink, please, it's been a long day."

"Yes sir." She scurried back through the door and he proceeded to the large table in the center of the great hall where he pointed to a chair "Sit here."

Shelley swallowed her retort for being treated as a trained dog; cautious now, she felt it wise not to rouse his anger again. They stared across the table at each other until Agnes returned accompanied by a younger woman. They placed a small platter of cold pork, a basket of warm bread and a bowl of fresh fruit upon the table. The younger woman put a pitcher and two glasses in front of him. "Will that be all sir?"

"Yes Ilsy." He replied as he continued his smug gaze at Shelley. "Shall we begin again?" He grabbed a loaf of bread and ripped off a piece. "Who are you?"

"I'm Shelley, who are you?"

"You really don't know? So you've entered my home to rob me just because you could?"

"I didn't come here to rob you; in fact, if you'll tell me where I am, I'll leave. Where am I?" She demanded, in a louder voice. Her eyes stared into his, matching their coldness with fire as hot as the one before them on the hearth.

"I see you persist in this game so we'll continue." He threw the bread back on the platter. "My name is Edward Nicholas Wodehouse and we sit in Wodegate Castle. Now it's your turn."

"I don't know why I'm here." She looked away from him as reality closed in.

"Touching story, but it doesn't work." His face flushed as he threatened her. "Tell me the real reason you're here or I'll call the sheriff and let him take you."

"When you first saw me, you referred to 'the rest'." Shelley said. "What did you mean?"

It was the final straw and his temper flared. "You don't get to ask questions of me; this is my home. You supply your identity and a plausible reason you're here or it's off you go!"

"Very well sir." She used the term loosely. "I'll attempt to tell you what I know, which isn't much..." Her voice faded for a moment before she gave her name. "I'm Shelley Lindquist from Atlanta, Georgia."

"From the States? Well, I understand your behavior now, Ms. Lindquist; state your purpose for being here."

"It isn't for the pleasure of your company, sir." Shelley left her chair. "This is going nowhere and I'll be leaving. Thank you for your warm hospitality, that is, Jakke's." Grabbing her purse, she gave Jakke a last pet and walked to the massive doors.

"Come back here!" Before Nicholas could reach her, she managed to drag one of the big doors half-open and wiggle through it sideways. He rushed around the large table to follow her and Jakke brushed past him.

Expecting to see the Shelley person running away, he found her motionless on the terrace, her bag on the ground beside her where it dropped, and her hand upon Jakke's shoulders.

She stared wordless over the green fields and forests of the large river valley in front of her. The orange sun set low behind smaller hills and distant mountains as it signaled the day's end and dipped beneath the horizon.

CHAPTER Three - Georgia to...

Wodegate Castle is a cold place Shelley thought and the gray stone of the castle does nothing to change that. She sat in her room, bundled in wool blankets before the fire.

Agnes brought her a proper dinner earlier after learning she hadn't eaten since breakfast. 'Sir' retired to his rooms after her attempted escape and offered no information on where she was or how she'd arrived.

Shelley felt certain he knew something; his remark about her difference from 'the rest' was strange and Agnes was silent to her questions, too. A knock on the door startled her from her thoughts.

"Yes?"

"I'm coming in so please cover yourself." Nicholas called through the door.

"I couldn't be more covered unless you added a rug." She opened the door.

He eyed the multiple blankets around her and the heavy wool socks on her feet. "Um, yes; may I enter?"

"It's your home; would it matter if I said no?" She returned to the bench before the fire.

He stood at the hearth to warm his hands. "We should try to resolve this issue."

"What issue?" Shelley said in exasperation. "That I'm here against my will or arrived by a means I don't understand?"

"Both; if we share our information you may understand your arrival better." Nicholas pulled a nearby stool to the fire. "Forces are at play beyond our control; I'll explain, but first I need to hear your story and what of your passage here."

"No, first I want to know where I am." Shelley corrected him and leaned forward in her impatience. "It's a great worry. You know where I'm from; at least do me the courtesy of relieving my mind."

He looked at her, "Wodegate Castle sits in the north of Scotland, fifty miles from the coast."

"Scotland. I suspected it earlier when I saw the countryside, but couldn't understand how it could be. What am I to do? My two boys are at home in Atlanta and need me. I have to get back." Her voice wavered. "Can I get back?"

Head in her hands, she tried to calm herself then fixed him in her gaze. "I'm a decorator in Atlanta. I visited a salvage shop just south of there. You or someone closely resembling you approached me. He led me to doors in an architectural collection from Europe — your doors on this castle; then disappeared. I love historical architecture and touched one of the lions' heads. When I did there was a flash of light, I lost consciousness and woke up inside your castle."

Nicolas listened carefully. "Describe this older man to me."

"Imagine yourself in fifty years; gray hair, wrinkles, paunch, walks with a limp."

"With a limp you say; left leg?" Nicholas knew who she'd seen.

"Yes, it was; how do you know that?"

"Come with me." He said and walked out the door.

"You have the manners of a goat." She said under her breath and threw off her blankets. With sandals over her socks, she followed as ordered. He stopped at the end of the passageway and flipped a light switch for the chandelier overhead.

"Recognize him?" He pointed to a life-size portrait on the wall.

"It's him, maybe; his clothing wasn't as grand and his hair was gray and shaggy."

"Your visitor was my great-grandfather, Edward Nicholas Wodehause, who lived long before us. He lost a leg during the War in America and had a wooden prosthesis which explains the limp in the man you saw. When he returned to Wodegate after the war, he found relatives had claimed the estate during his long absence. He spent his last remaining days on pension, trying to recover ownership, but was unsuccessful."

"You're telling me he's a ghost?" Shelley said in disbelief. "I've trusted in many things, but never ghosts and don't intend to start now. Tell me another story 'sir' because this one doesn't, as you once said to me, 'work'."

He turned off the light. "Are you hungry?"

"Agnes brought food earlier, but I could drink something hot; it's freezing in here." She shivered a great toes-to-nose shiver that warned she needed her blankets back.

He led the way downstairs to the kitchen. "You should have worn warmer clothing."

"Yes, since I knew I'd be in Scotland by the end of the day." She said under her breath and thought 'is this man for real?'

He heard her remark and realized she had no way of knowing she'd be here, but his pang of guilt lasted only a few seconds. Should I tell her why she's here and that she isn't the first? He kept silent and entered the kitchen where Shelley walked straight to the hearth's side to warm her feet.

"We have chocolate; or do you prefer tea?" Nicolas put water on the gas stove and helped himself to the last of the day's coffee.

"Tea, please." Shelley wondered when she'd be able to get home. "How can I call my mother and tell her I'm in Scotland? I'm so confused."

Nicholas put a cup of tea on the small bench beside her. "The truth is that your presence is due to Edward's vow to assist his descendants until Wodegate is restored to the family. That 'family' is me, his last remaining heir. If he's unsuccessful, Wodegate will remain with the man who hired me to manage the estate."

"But what does that have to do with me? I need to get home; my boys will worry if I'm not back by Sunday."

Nicholas stared at her. "Sunday?"

"Yes, three days from now; I arrived on Thursday and have to be home by Sunday. Mom, Mark and Jason expect me and I won't disappoint them." His face was blank and unreadable. "What?" Shelley said.

He retrieved a calendar from the wall and gave it to her. "This may explain."

She looked for Sunday, but the days were off then she noticed the year. "This is an old calendar for 2011, no wonder I can't find the correct date." He remained silent and she tried again. "This calendar is old, the correct year is 2016."

"The correct year is 2011, Mrs. Lindquist, August 21, 2011 to be exact."

"But that means...I'm miles from home...and in the past."

"Yes." He confirmed. "I'm sorry, there's nothing I can do to change it."

Her eyes clouded up and her head dropped to her hands. Then she looked at him before turning away. "I'll go to my room now."

"Yes, sleep will help." Nicholas said.

Shelley gave him a look over her shoulder meant to kill. "I doubt it, unless I awake and find this a nightmare. Good night."

After she left, Nicholas poured scotch into his coffee and sat watching the fire until it burned low. I'm thirty-six years old, unmarried and no children. Why are you doing this to me, Edward? What's so important on this estate that you can't rest and why keep sending these strangers?

Half-expecting a ghostly voice, he sipped his coffee. Only the wind replied as it stole past the panes and drafty doors of the castle like strings on a distant violin. He raised his cup to his long-lost host then took the lonely walk to his room.

Shelley stayed awake most of the night trying to find a solution; she paced and kept the fire on the hearth burning before falling asleep in the early hours. The sun was up when she awoke and the room, damp-cold. She cast an eye to the hearth and confirmed the fire was out and the wood box, empty.

Pulling a blanket from the big bed to the deep ledge at the window, she sat wrapped in its warmth and stared at the scene before her. A low-lying ground fog lay in the river valley as the sun rose, but it began to lift as daylight came. The only thing clear is I'm stuck here; she pulled the blanket closer... at least until Grandfather Wodehause releases me back to my life? She still couldn't believe that part.

Memories of her boys and mother were constantly on her mind; the possibilities were endless and beyond understanding. At first, the unthinkable fear preyed on her that the boys didn't exist anymore. But she thought it out last night; they were born in 2003 and already existed in 2011 Atlanta. "Does this even work that way?" She wondered aloud.

At that moment, Agnes knocked, "Miss? I have something for ye."

"Come in, Agnes."

She entered with her arms full of clothing. "These belonged to my daughter when she was yer size. You might like them, at least until ye can buy yer own."

Shelley helped her empty her arms onto the bed. "Thank you Agnes, you're very thoughtful."

"Ye're welcome; I know it hasn't been easy since yer arrival and bein cold is niver fun. There are wool sweaters and jeans and here's a perfectly good coat and scarf in case ye want a walk-about. The extra wellies are downstairs at the back kitchen door, I'm sure ye'll be able to find yer size."

"Agnes, you don't how much I appreciate this."

She smiled at her. "My daughter lives in Edinburgh noo with her husband and we get ta see each other on holiday and in the summer. Oh, I brought a toothbrush, shampoo and other things ye might be needin in this bag. Breakfast is ready downstairs when ye are."

After she left, Shelley picked something warm to wear and cleaned up before dressing. It's been a long twenty-four hours, thank-goodness for Agnes. Obviously, 'sir' didn't think of any of this, not even a toothbrush.

A pair of jeans, a long-sleeved shirt, sweater and sneakers made her feel better and warmer. She found the stairs to the kitchen where both Agnes and Ilsa were busy at their work. The large wooden table was covered with fresh vegetables; potatoes, carrots and greens.

"These are lovely. Do you grow them here?"

"Yes Miss, out back in the garden. Yer welcome to help yourself to any ye enjoy." Ilsa said.

Agnes wiped her hands on her apron, "Ye'll be needin breakfast first; what do ye like? We have fresh eggs, bread, oatmeal, what can I fix fer ye?"

"Eggs and toast would be heaven." Shelley searched for a pan at the stove, but Agnes joined her.

"I'll do that Miss, sit and they'll be ready in a jiff."

"Sorry, I'm not used to being waited on. I'm usually the one at the stove on school mornings." Her attention drifted; Agnes and Ilsa noticed and looked at each other.

Ilsa came to lead her to the table. "Now, not to worry, I'm sure ye'll get all sorted out and soon be back with yer family."

"All of what?" Nicholas appeared at the door. Ilsa's eyes dropped and she returned to the work table.

Agnes took over; "A little chit-chat tween women sir, nothin to concern yourself with. I'll get those eggs for ye Miss, and you sir?"

"A scone and coffee will be fine Agnes. And how are you this morning Mrs. Lindquist? I see you have warm clothes today."

"Yes, Agnes was nice enough to bring me a few of her daughter's clothes this morning and personal items like toothpaste; she's very thoughtful that way." Shelley emphasized the last part intending he understand her opinion of his thoughtlessness.

He took a seat and was apparently oblivious to her opinions. "Will you take a ride with me after breakfast? You should see the estate and become better acquainted with the area." He glanced at the two servants busy at their work. "You have an idea of what's at stake in the subject discussed yesterday and we can speak freely outside the castle."

Shelley looked at him, trying to decide whether she could trust him and measure his true intent. No matter, she thought, I need to get out for a while. "Yes, I'd enjoy that."

She stood outside the kitchen door waiting until Nicholas came from the stable with two fine horses, a chestnut mare and a large, black gelding. Jakke trotted along behind until he spotted Shelley and broke into a run; he managed a quick, sloppy kiss before she could take evasive action.

"Jakke!" Nicholas called the hound to his side.

Shelley approached the mare and let her sniff her hand then stroked her nose and neck. "I used to ride with my parents." He said nothing and concentrated on the black's bridle. She remembered a scene in her childhood when she rode her new pony out of the barn. Both parents followed her on their horses and they took the path together to the park.

As Nicholas calmed his horse, he asked, "Ready?"

They followed a trail to the top of the hill behind the castle and stopped to look out over the open forest ahead. She saw again the river flanked by green hills below them; shame I can't enjoy this as a tourist, the boys would love it. Remembering her boys thousands of miles away... years away, was all too much and a tear rolled down her cheek before she could catch it. She angrily wiped it away and followed him as both horses, familiar with the trail, took them into the woods.

The bridle path wound through old-growth fir trees noisy with birds and squirrels; oak and ash wore their fall colors and dropped leaves of every color in their way. Shelley drank in the beauty comparing it to her home then remembered Atlanta's maples wouldn't turn for weeks. Mark and Jason again entered her mind and the yearning to see them weighed heavily upon her.

Nicholas watched her from his horse. "It's hard to believe there were no trees here at one time; forests were leveled for firewood and building purposes by the mid-17th century. Most of this was reforested by my great-grandfather Edward's family. After their deaths, Wodegate came to him as the eldest and he continued to follow his father's example, up to the time he left for war."

"Who're the owners now?" Shelley said.

"Wilson Bailey inherited it a few years ago. He and his family live in Glasgow; he's in the steel industry." Nicholas looked away to a nearby stream. "Let's give the horses a drink and stretch our legs."

He dismounted and leaned against a large boulder at the water's edge. "What do you think of the estate so far?"

Shelley dismounted and led her horse to the water's edge. "It's beautiful here and quiet; I'm used to the noise of the city."

He smiled for the first time since she'd arrived. "Yes, I feel the same way. You see why this place is important to Edward and me; it isn't just its monetary value."

"You mean Edward, your dead grandfather."

He straightened at her remark. "You have a direct way of speaking Mrs. Lindquist and cut straight to the heart in a moment's time, therefore I'll be brief. Wilson Bailey wishes to sell this estate next year and 'cash in' on what you see. He owns a chunk of the steel plate industry, but steel in Scotland has undergone a downward trend. In his mind, steel is a much worthier project than keeping an old warrior like Wodegate alive." Nicholas went to the black and led him from the stream.

"My grandfather may be deceased, Mrs. Lindquist, but he dwells here on this estate. He's sent me two people since I arrived; one, an architect who specialized in ancient dwellings, returned home after uncovering nothing. The other is you and I confess I'm not sure of his reasons. Do you have any idea?"

"None; except that the old man was very interested when I mentioned father was a renovation architect." Shelley said.

Nicholas thought about it for a moment. "That may make sense in view of the circumstances under which Edward lost the estate. There were laws at the time which enabled family members to claim land and property if the owner was absent and left no direction.

In the case of death with no will or heir, they could present their genealogy link and prove their case in Court."

He looked back to the stream. "Edward's Will was never found; I believe it may be here, but well-hidden. He was a military man, structured and organized. It's unfathomable he'd leave before providing for the castle's upkeep and its business affairs; chance of death was great and he would not go into battle that way, I feel certain." Nicholas looked straight at her. "He'll wander this place until things are set right."

"You haven't explained why I'm here." She said. "Interior design with moderate knowledge of architectural design and blueprint reading hardly qualifies me to search for legal documents in castles. That is what you're hinting?"

"Yes, it is."

She made her point. "I remind you I was taken without permission; this is unfair and cruel treatment and I want to know when I'll be returned home."

"I'm not the one to ask that of and had nothing to do with bringing you here." Nicholas turned away to mount his horse. "Perhaps you should open your closed mind to the possibilities." Shelley opened her mouth to speak, but he held up his hand. "Edward holds the cards for your return; it might be to your advantage to communicate with him."

"And how can I do that?" She asked as she climbed onto the mare.

"I suggest you start somewhere, maybe a visit to the castle's library. I found a few of his letters there while cleaning out damaged books. At least give it a try Mrs. Lindquist; what do you have to lose?"

His voice remained detached and that was fine with her. Despite his belligerence, he believed what he was telling her, that much was clear. Should she work to solve the matter versus wasting energy on disbelief?

"Alright, I'll visit the library, walk the castle, and hold séances..." His eyebrows raised and a crease appeared between them.

She realized her levity was not well received. "Sorry, I will give Edward the benefit of the doubt. What other choice do I have?" She asked in hope Nicholas knew other options.

"None, to my knowledge; shall we ride further?" He said. "The river isn't far from here and it's one of the estate's largest assets."

"I'll take a raincheck; I need to readjust my anatomy to riding again."

"Ah, understood." He quashed a smile. "It's time you called me Nicholas; that is, if you wish."

Shelley took the mare's reins. "We'll see."

The little mare sensed a dry stall and share of oats ahead of her and responded with a hasty trot in the direction of the stables.

CHAPTER Four – New Belief

A hot bath would help Shelley's aching muscles, many of which were previously unknown to her before the morning's ride. Agnes and Ilsa carried the metal tub to Shelley's room and brought water to heat in the large pot hanging in the fireplace. This is a trip Shelley thought and remembered she was lucky to get a hot bath at all, considering Mr. Bailey was uninterested in updating the castle to modern times.

Nicholas' indifference flourished while they rode together, though he did clarify the reason she was here. No matter how much she wanted to be home with her family, she had trouble believing it was under a ghostly spirit's control. The fear of never returning preyed on her and she fought to overcome it by pushing it into the deepest corner of her mind whenever possible.

Also of worry was a question born of selfish curiosity; what did Nicholas plan to do if the estate sells? If marooned here, she became his responsibility wanted or not and with his present detachment, he might turn her out and walk away. Panic continued to rise as she realized Wodegate was important to her future, too.

She set out to explore the castle in its cool, dusty-dampness after dressing in a heavier sweater. The Bailey's hadn't installed central heat either, a sure sign to her their plan had always been to sell.

On the way through the upstairs passageways, she stopped again to study Edward's portrait. "You were a handsome man in your day." She noticed his eyes were hazel, the same as Nicholas' when he'd looked at her on the mare.

She took the stone steps down to the large kitchen where a simmering pot hung in the fireplace. Were it not for the modern gas stove, this place is an ideal medieval movie setting she thought. Ilsa stood at the massive work table kneading some dough but looked up at Shelley and smiled.

"Something smells delicious."

"Tis lamb stew for dinner, mam, we do it on the fire; the wood smoke adds to the taste."

"I can't wait. Can you tell me where to find wood to restock my fire tonight?"

Ilsa wiped her floury hands on her apron. "I'd be glad to fetch it for you, let me clean off my hands first. The apples are delicious this year so Agnes and I decided on an apple pie for dessert."

"Mmm, it's one of my favorites. Please, continue what you're doing and point me in the right direction."

"If you're sure Mam?" Shelley nodded. "Then thank-you; the wood is outside this door and to the right" Ilsa said. "There's a canvas bag to carry with, too."

Shelley pushed through the back door, the air outside felt good and she lingered to let the sun warm her face. She closed her eyes for a second and imagined being home under the southern sky again then returned to reality and descended the steps to a neat stack of kindling against the kitchen wall.

Nicholas approached from the stables. "Can I help?"

"I'm fine here." She started gathering a few pieces into the bag.

"Very well." He passed by her into the kitchen, but reappeared, catching the door in mid-swing. "At least let me carry it up the stairs for you."

"Very well." She echoed him on purpose, but her eyes betrayed her.

"Ah. I'm told I'm too short with people; you use my own words against me?"

"Could be." Shelley threw one last piece into the canvas bag. "This should keep me warm tonight." Nicholas grabbed the bag and she followed him upstairs.

"Do you have time to show me the library?" She asked after he'd laid the fire on the hearth.

"Do you want to go there now?" He said.

"Perfect." Nicholas led her to the west end of the castle where they descended a circular stone staircase, barely the width of his shoulders, into the first-floor library.

He began to pull open the heavy drapes over the windows. "I think Edward spent time here, judging from the number of books and letters with his name inscribed; his room is above us near the stairs we took."

She looked at the shelves covering every inch of wall space, even over windows and the door. Several track ladders stood at the ready for high reaching.

"This library is amazing." She strained to see the books' titles in the dimness; the four windows shed scant light through their slots in the thick stone wall and there were candle chandeliers hanging from the ceiling. "You don't use the candles for light here, do you?"

"No, we do this." He turned to flip a wall-switch and lights appeared in several areas around the massive room.

"It's beautiful!" She said. The fireplace mantel had lamps at both ends and a large desk and two lounge chairs each had their own reading lamps. Indirect lighting bathed the walls and the high-beamed ceiling, revealing the room's striking stone and beam construction.

Nicholas glanced at her. "I came to work on the estate in 2002 and reading was an important part of my life; the lighting in here was terrible and Bailey wasn't interested in any improvements, so I used my own funds. I left the candelabras intact as part of the castle's history."

"Spanish wrought iron aren't they and difficult to replicate."

He showed new interest. "Yes, there's much Spanish influence here due to the nearby seaport; my early grandfathers traded grain and wool."

She browsed the lower bookshelves as Nicholas pulled a large packet from a desk drawer.

"Allow me to show you a letter I found then I'll leave you to your own space." He emptied the packet's contents. "These are dated between 1770 and 1771, before Edward left."

Shelley picked up one of the folded parchment letters with gentle hands. Portions of sealing wax still remained on the paper. "Is this part of Edward's family seal?" She asked. 'Wodehause' was readable, but the writer's initials were missing. "What was Edward's father's name?"

He glanced at the letter. "Christian Nicholas."

She opened the folded paper while he continued to sort through the others. "It's in surprising condition for its age."

"These were inside a large edition of Shakespeare on one of the higher shelves, Edward's private safe for valued documents I suspect." Nicholas found the letter he searched for and handed it to her. "This is interesting."

She read aloud: *My dear son Edward*. Her eyes brightened. "It's from Edward's mother."

Nicholas saw her enthusiasm. "Yes, she often wrote to him."

Shelley read more: *Your father and I have so far suffered none of the terrible sickness that threatens so many in nearby London. We keep to ourselves and pray that will be enough. Your brother wrote from the farm and they are well. I worry because of their position; they have few assets and nothing to fall back on. Will is a good farmer but they rent the farm and house and I pray they stay solvent as we cannot aid him financially, should something befall them.*

"I see what you mean; she brings up William's money problems." Shelley said.

"Yes, if something beset them, such as the great clearance of estate farms for sheep-raising around that time, it could be the motive for their focus on Wodegate during Edward's absence."

Shelley folded the letter and gave it back to him. "If we trace the genealogy and history from William, we might get a better understanding of his claim on Wodegate. People do unexpected things in desperate times; do you have a current genealogy document for your side of the family?"

He walked to a nearby shelf and retrieved a round leather case. "This is something I commissioned several years ago with a genealogist in London." He pulled out a rolled parchment tied with ribbon, spread it open on the desk and placed glass paperweights to keep it flat. "You can see my eighth-removed grandfather Christian Wodehause here, his sons Edward and William here."

She studied the family tree. "Do you have the legal documents turning the estate over to William?"

"I do not." He was tired of that answer and knew everything came down to it. He rerolled the parchment, his frustration obvious.

"Surely, the original copy lies with a government bureau?" She said. "I don't know how it works here, but at home, each county has file books dating back to colonial days of each person's property and how it changed hands since first surveyed."

Nicholas' impatience flared. "Your country is slightly over two hundred years old, a mere 'youngster' compared to ours. In addition, borders, governments and courts have shifted since the castle's origin. But yes, you're right, somewhere documents may exist, it's just a matter of finding them."

He changed the subject to a more pleasant one. "Shall we visit the kitchen and persuade Ilsa to part with a piece of apple pie before tonight's dinner?"

She knew their talk was over but she planned to return later. "Throw in a cup of coffee and I'm there." His face relaxed, but she didn't trust his moodiness. There was a wall between them and she didn't understand his innate habit of distancing himself.

Later, after Ilsa and Agnes left, Shelley sat in one of the library's big overstuffed chairs. The fire blazed and she kept a tartan blanket over her shoulders against the castle's coolness. Compiling a list of known facts on Wodegate and its history for her own use, she wrote the names of Nicholas's ancestors; the founders Christian and his wife Anne, Edward, his birth date and service with Frazer's Highlanders, and finally, his brother William. Ironic that genealogy hadn't been among her interests before, because she found it fascinating now.

She considered Nicholas' suggestion to acknowledge Edward; might the old ghost send her home if she continued the search for him? Her smile faded as she realized she didn't have any idea how to contact him and needed a plan. The lateness of the night and the warmth of the fire soon took their toll and she drifted off to sleep.

"Ay lass, ye dae need a plan."

She stirred at the words and thought Edward stood before her. 'I must be dreaming.'

"Nay, ye not be dreamin girl. Din you wish ta talk? Here A am, speak while ye can. A don't have all nicht."

"Edward!" She sat up to look at him through wide eyes. "You're here, I mean, good evening, sir. You're looking much improved from the last time we met in the warehouse."

"A played a part so we'd not attract undue attention; A couldna wear this outfit in 'Atlanta, Georgia' now could A?"

In full military regalia he stood; his kilt of Blackwatch tartan, a fine red jacket adorned with gold epaulets, flintlock pistol tucked into his belt, basket-weave sword and black feathers atop his dark blue bonnet.

She tried to find a suitable response to the life-size ghost before her. "No, I suppose not." His mouth was a straight line as he stared at her. "I mean — no sir."

He suppressed a smile and was brusque with his reply. "Days be past when people respectit me as they did in Frazer's Regiment. A simple 'Edward' will do noo. What hae ye found tae help Nicholas?"

She showed him the copy of his mother's letter. "We believe your brother William and his wife encountered financial difficulties around the period you were overseas in 1776."

Edward glanced at the letter. "Ay, the landowner sold oot tae a lairge farm leavin them homeless and wi'out a living. Poor Will'am, destitute and his wife a shrew; she drove im to bring her and their five bairns ta Wodegate."

Shelley tried to think of her most pertinent questions, knowing time with him might be short. "Did you leave a will or a trust before you sailed for the colonies?"

His face turned dark. "D-ye think I'm daft wummin? I could niver leave wi'out ensurin the estate's safety and left a Will and Trust by solicitor."

"Nicholas and I thought as much."

"Ye do? Then why ask?" His look was penetrating.

"I had to confirm it; a search is a waste of time otherwise...sir. Did you leave a copy somewhere?"

"Och ay, both left wi Arden Ross, my groundskeeper; a true friend who lived over the stables. A trustit him t'bide my return, and documents were sent to Willum by messenger afore I sailed. An noo lass, A must leave, it's difficult for me ta linger so."

Shelley panicked. "Wait, I'll pass this along to Nicholas, but please, tell me I might go home now. My boys are without parents and I don't want them to grow up that way."

He looked at her. "It's no way for weans to thrive, Nicholas is proof of that. Home it be lass, but bide one day, to give yer room to settle things here wi' him. Noo it's goodbye. Should ye need me, clear yer mind and call; I'll come if I can."

Edward was gone before her eyes; a vision, a vapor, there and then not. It took a few minutes to stop trembling before she pulled herself plus blanket out of the chair. Edward's words 'bide one day' rang in her head as she walked up the stairs. Did she trust him... what choice did she have?

CHAPTER Five - Time

The next morning, Shelley followed a gravel pathway from the kitchen garden to the large stable which sat behind the castle. She walked through the high double doors and noticed Nicholas, his tee shirt wet and jeans muddy as he tended the black stallion.

"Good morning."

"Good morning." He barely glanced at her.

"May I speak with you?" Shelley approached the mare in her stall and rubbed her nose.

"Yes, what is it?"

"Edward paid a visit to the library last night; would you like to hear about it?"

He dropped the hard brush in a bucket. "Let's go upstairs to the office." He left the black tied to a stall and motioned for her to come. She couldn't help but feel she'd been trained like Jakke, but followed him up the well-worn steps to the door at the top.

The room was open the length of the stable, its ceiling high-pitched to the thatched roof. Cobwebs draped the wooden beams where saddles and tack hung over many in sporadic fashion. Pictures of horses, old framed newspaper clippings and ribbons clung to the walls and the office smelled of hay dust, leather and saddle soap. Sunshine entered through several windows on both sides of the room, but diminished by their dirty panes.

Nicholas wiped off two chairs. "Sorry for the dust up here; I should ask Agnes to give it some attention. It's hard with only the three of us, there's other work more important than this office."

Shelley walked around the room to look at the pictures before taking a seat. "How many horses lived here?"

"In its heyday, at least twenty; that included those for carriages, farm work and a few for riding; now we keep the two. What have you found out?"

"Edward left a will and trust papers in the hands of his estate manager, one Arden Ross, in fact this office was where Mr. Ross lived. Edward also delivered a copy by messenger to William before he sailed for the colonies."

"I knew it." Nicholas arose in his excitement. "Did he say where the papers are?"

"I don't think Edward remembers; it seems some of his life has faded... in, ah... his 'present condition'. Mr. Ross was Edward's trusted friend; he would have kept them in a safe place, perhaps even in this building."

She hesitated then gave him her other news. "There's something else; Edward is sending me home to my boys today, at my request."

The news caught him unawares and he sat down again. His instinct was to say she couldn't leave, but it would hold no threat now she'd talked to Edward.

"I'm sorry to hear it; having you here was ... refreshing for all of us and gave new life to the place." He stood up and turned to open the door. "Shall we go downstairs? I have chores to finish."

"Yes, of course." Surprised by his abrupt reaction and yet not, she realized Nicholas never opened himself to anyone, why would he now?

At the foot of the stairs she tried to extend the conversation. "Perhaps we'll see each other later at dinner."

He picked up the discarded brush and looked at her. "Yes, perhaps." His demeanor expressed closure and dismissal as he returned to the stallion's care.

As soon as she left, Nicholas dropped his forehead against the black's warm flank. Edward's voice asked inside him, "Are ye going to let the bonnie lass go wi'out tellin her?"

Nicholas retorted, "Edward, you do not get to direct me in matters of the heart, I won't stand for it, do you hear?" No answer came back as usual.

The one-way conversations began years ago and he'd wound up at Wodegate because of Edward's voice in his head. He'd been content with his law practice in Aberdeen, but had to give it up when Edward began talking to him during court proceedings. Mr. Bailey posted an estate manager position in the newspaper shortly after that; Nicholas introduced himself and got the job. It was all a calculated move of Edward's to bring him inside the estate to look for the Will.

Edward began bringing people to him the following year and Nicholas's jealousy flared. He thought his grandfather favored a stranger due to a lack of faith in him. It was childish, but typical; Nicholas was an only child born to parents too busy to raise him. He entered boarding school at the age of five and over the years developed into a stand-alone child, able to handle bullies and conform to the school's rules. As an adult, he depended only upon himself, as he was taught.

He started to question his solitary lifestyle for the first time when Shelley arrived and admired her logic and ability to adjust to circumstances beyond her control. She was the first to make him see himself as others did; perhaps if she stayed he thought, but it was too late for that now.

He patted the black's withers and led him back to the paddock muttering "I've accomplished nothing again."

Edward's clear reply came at once to him; "Except to let the lass into your heart."

Shelley sat on the window ledge looking one last time over the rolling pastures of the river valley. Scotland is breath-taking she thought; I hope to return under better circumstances someday.

The clothes Agnes gave her lay folded on the bed and she left nothing behind except the flowers picked beside the stream where she and Nicolas watered the horses.

Clearing her mind of all thoughts, she called out "Edward."

He came in a few minutes. "Are ye ready lass?"

"Yes, but one moment before we go. Will you take care of Nicholas? He seems so lonely and afraid to reach out...to anyone."

"Ay, I will." He offered his hand and she took it.

CHAPTER Six- Home Again

Mark helped Grams get supper ready by stirring the mashed potatoes while his brother Jason put the dishes and silverware on the table.

Dinner was earlier with their mother on vacation. She usually worked until five or six every night and arrived home later, depending on traffic. Not that they starved or anything; she always made sure there was plenty of food in the fridge.

Their favorite part of the day was meeting her at the front door; Jason would take her briefcase and she hugged them before asking the latest news from school. They loved her because she'd been there for them every day since their dad left for Hong Kong. Secretly, Mark intended to be there for her after he grew up, too.

"How do these look, Grams?" Mark said.

Janet gave the potatoes a trial stir. "Chef-quality - set them on the table and we'll eat. Jason, wash your hands."

"Already did." He said.

"Ok, I'm taking that for truth. Let's sit shall we? So how was school today, boys?" She salt and peppered the mashed potatoes then handed them to Mark who took a large helping.

"School was good; I aced the math test today."

"Your studies last night paid off. Jason, how was your day?"

He passed the chicken. "It was okay; I got a C on the science test."

Jason didn't enjoy school like Mark did; kids are never alike Janet thought and smiled at him. "Do your best, Jason, that's what we expect. Looks like you have some studying to do before the next one; if either of you need extra help be sure to ask, okay?"

"Yes mam."

"When's mom coming home?" Jason said.

"She'll be home Sunday, and this old lady can get some rest. I love you both and wouldn't have missed this for anything, but have mercy, you guys have energy!"

The phone rang and Janet rushed to pick it up.

"Hi mom." Shelley said.

"Hi dear! We wondered when you'd be home. Are you nearby?" The boys pushed their way nearer. "Hush, I can't hear your mother."

The sweet commotion was music to her ears; Shelly soaked it up then fibbed. "I left later than planned and won't make it for another hour. Eat without me; I should be there around eight. Those kids behaving for you?"

"Oh, they've been perfect dears. Just get here safely." Janet said.

"Ok, mom, love you guys..."

"Love you, too." They all said.

She knew they were safe now. It was bizarre being back; one moment she was sitting by the castle window, the next, leaving the warehouse for her car. Watching people on the street for a few minutes helped her to be less disoriented before she started the drive home.

The boys came running across the porch as she drove into the driveway.

"Mom!" They attached themselves to her and brought her through the front door.

Janet came from the kitchen. "Well, how was your trip? Did you see any treasures you liked at the warehouse?"

"Oh, many things, but we'll talk later. I need to unwind and enjoy being home."

"Of course dear, you must be worn out from the drive. Are you hungry, I saved you dinner?"

Meanwhile, son Jason let loose of his mother's waist with a hopeful grin. "Did you bring us something?"

Shelley dropped a kiss on each boy's head. "Let me get my bag upstairs first."

Her room felt strange; how small it was compared to the one she'd occupied the last two nights, but it's mine and warmer. She removed two sacks from her luggage bought at a roadside stand and took them to the boys.

"Ok guys, here you go, straight from Alligator Willies' Roadside Rest."

Mark and Jason ripped open their bags and exclaimed in delight. "Cool. Awesome!"

"You asked for claws and I aim to please." Personally, Shelley thought them detestable; alligator claws on keychains... yuck. But to ten-year-old boys in Georgia, they were the best gift ever.

In the kitchen, she poured a large glass of milk and plated a piece of her mother's meatloaf. "Mmm, I missed this."

Janet smiled at her. "You were only away one week, dear."

"It seemed much longer... and farther away. I didn't bring you a claw, sorry." Shelley grinned at her.

Janet rolled her eyes and took her plate to the sink. "Oh please, consider it a positive. What do you mean it seemed longer; did you enjoy your getaway?"

Shelley searched for the right words. "It was unlike any trip I've ever taken."

"Really, in what way?" Janet said.

"It's hard to describe."

"Try me!" Janet looked too eager and focused on her daughter.

Shelley recognized the signs; she thinks I met someone, if only it were that simple. "I'm saying this once as clearly as possible. If you doubt me, I want your promise not to call our family doctor or tell anyone else."

"Alright, my lips are sealed." Janet made a motion of zipping her lips.

"How old are we, Mom, ten?"

"Just tell me; I'll understand. You want coffee?"

"Please. So I'm in the warehouse, a fantastic place full of furnishings and re-purposed treasures. I visited a room with hundreds of doors of every sort displayed. An old gentleman, whom I assumed worked there, took me to a pair of doors from a castle. They were impressive, at least twelve feet tall and solid wood with fancy lions-head hardware." She stopped because she pictured them as they were at Wodegate.

"Go on," Janet said. "What happened next?"

"I touched one and went somewhere."

"What do you mean; you left the room?" Janet said.

"I left, but in a different way; one minute I was there, the next in a huge castle... in Scotland." Shelley waited to see what her mother had to say.

Janet looked at her. "Okay, I'm processing."

"Look Mom, I'm not under the influence, it's the truth. I've been in Scotland for the past three days trying to help find papers that can return an estate to its rightful heir."

"And you reached Scotland how?"

"I was transported there... by a ghost, Edward Wodehause, an earlier owner of Wodegate Estate. His seventh-removed grandson, Nicholas, now lives there as the estate's manager. He's the rightful heir, but needs to find Edward's lost Will from 1776 to prove it."

"The year the War of Independence began." Janet said.

Shelley couldn't discern her mother's reaction; heck, she wouldn't believe the story herself. "This is a lot I know; I'm asking you not to interpret it as a nightmare or reaction to a food allergy."

"It would be easier that way." Janet put on a half-smile. "But if you tell me you magically transported to Scotland for a few days, I believe you dear. You appear perfectly normal otherwise; if anyone could do something so crazy... um... out of the ordinary, it's my daughter."

Shelley drew her mom into a hug. "Thanks Mom for having faith in me."

"Not so fast; is that it?" Janet scrutinized her with raised eyebrows. "No forthcoming adventures as a result of this brief interlude in your life?"

"No, it ended when I returned to Atlanta." Shelley's voice faded with the finality of the words; she questioned silently, do I have regrets?

Janet knew her daughter too well, her expression showed unrest, but she decided to ignore it for now. "Good. I'll keep your secret, but others might not be able to if 'they' get wind of it." Mark came around the corner and Janet nodded toward him.

"Mom, these sneakers are coming loose around the soles, see?" He held up a foot to wiggle his toes.

"Okay, tomorrow after school. Jason?" She called upstairs. "We're going shoe-shopping tomorrow; how are yours?"

Jason came to the upstairs landing. "You mean these?" His shoe had a sole flapping, too; Shelley gave a resigned sigh. "Ok, I'm picking you both up tomorrow."

Janet put her arms around her. "It's nice to have you back, dear."

"Thanks Mom, it's good to be here. I'm beat and going to bed. Boys, I'm coming up to tuck you in and you better be in bed by the time I get there." After the usual stall tactics, both Mark and Jason settled into their beds.

Shelley reached her own bed and at last pulled the covers up; whispering to her pillow "I've missed you", she took a deep breath, exhaled and relaxed.

"Shelley lass." Just a memory she told herself as she turned over and punched her pillow into shape.

"Lass!"

"What?" Shelley sat up abruptly to look around. "Why are you calling me?"

Then she heard a light tap at her door. "Are you okay dear?" Janet said.

"Yes Mother, I'm fine, good night."

She fell back and closed her eyes, but sensed someone in her room. "Mom, I told you..."

"Faith, your mum is bonnie. Tis clear where her bairn teuk her looks." Edward stood before the foot of the bed in all his glory.

"What are you doing?" Shelley whispered. "We can't talk here, you'll wake my family."

"Then where lassie? I have news from Nicholas at Wodegate."

"Not anywhere; we were done when I returned. You're not supposed to zap in and out whenever you want." She straightened the covers until her curiosity got the best of her. "You're here, what is it?"

"The lad is in sorry shape... he didnae tell you how he feels; he feart ye'd think him daft." Edward removed his blue military bonnet.

"How he feels... about me?" Shelley said. "I know well his feelings—cold and empty. He made that plain, and I kept aloof as he wished. Now go away Edward, we're done here." With that, she threw the covers over her head and pretended to sleep. Silence ensued and after a suitable pause, she pulled the sheet from one eye to confirm his absence. But he remained at the foot of the bed, perusing the room's furnishings with an innocent air while he waited.

"URRRR!" Shelley threw off the covers. "What do you suggest, Edward?"

"Hae compassion for one, and a plan. Dae yer searchin from here intae those boxes yer always pickin away at..."

Shelley corrected him. "Computers, Edward."

"Ay, compooters. Find ma papers, bring em to Nicholas; solve his problems wi Wodegate and gi him anither chance."

"What's wrong with him coming here if he's so besotted? I have a life and can't drop everything to meet his whims."

"Lass, wiye juist think aboot it?"

"Good night Edward." She said.

Janet and the boys cleared out of the hall where they'd gathered to listen. "Shhh... go on, get back to bed," Janet motioned them away with a whisper and jumped into her room just as Shelley opened her door and walked downstairs.

After waiting for the boys to settle, Janet found her at the kitchen counter with a glass of milk and a stack of chocolate chip cookies. "Those look good; save a few for me."

"What are you doing up Mom? You didn't hear..." Janet nodded. "Oh Mom, I'm sorry."

"Why? I've heard the basic story; this just confirms you're not crazy and neither am I for believing you. Now scoot over and get real with me; who is this Edward?"

By the time Shelley filled her in on the details i.e. Wodegate, Nicholas and Edward, the clock struck four-thirty and the bag of cookies was empty.

"That's a real story, dear." Janet carried both their glasses to the sink. "What now?"

"I don't know Mom, work is 8 to 5; I can't spend hours researching an obscure estate in northern Britain from hundreds of years ago."

"Well, that too, but I wasn't referring to legal papers." Janet said. "This Nicholas, is he handsome?"

"It's not like that." Shelley dunked one more cookie and took a bite.

"Ah, so he is." Janet suppressed her smile.

"He tolerated me the entire time and couldn't wait until I left." Shelley took a sip of milk. "When we last spoke I told him I was leaving; he described my visit as 'refreshing' and he had to get back to his chores."

Janet cast a knowing look her way. "Shelley, your father was a warm, sweet man, but when he tried to talk of love, he froze up like a glacier in January. This Scotsman sounds like he has the same problem; don't be so quick to judge."

"All right, let's say I find the documents; how do I get them to him? He's in the past. I can't just jump on a jet and fly there. Besides, it was five years ago we met and the estate was to be sold in 2012..." She straightened. "The estate may be gone."

"Where are you going?" Janet said.

"To my laptop to look up the castle." Shelley called from the stairs.

Janet followed her. "No way am I missing out on this." She glanced at her watch and knocked on the boys' door as she passed; "Time to get up guys—school."

Shelley entered 'Wodegate Castle Scotland' to the computer as Janet arrived. The browser found a link that drew her attention. "Wodegate Estate Ownership Contested" the article read; the date was January 21, 2012. "This only leaves a few months to gather research and return it to 2011."

Janet overheard and leaned over her shoulder. "We can do it, if you let me help, dear."

Shelley jerked at her unexpected voice. "Jeeesh, Mom, give me warning. Absolutely not! It's enough I'm involved in this ghostly mystery meets time-travel. I will not involve my family. Who knows what could happen?"

"We can't know for sure." Janet said. "Maybe you'll solve someone's problem, restore a long-lost inheritance... find romance in an otherwise staid lifestyle?"

Shelley, with a recalled teenage rebuttal of 'Oh Mother' at the ready, paused to remember a few instances Janet had been right. There was the time she'd decided not to listen to her mother and dated Harry Dixon, a total dud; then another, when she decided to do her own demo on her first apartment, luckily the fire department arrived within minutes of her 911 call.

"Okay, you may be right, Mom." Shelley said. "But promise me one thing; no time-travel unless we're together."

Janet thought, that'll be the day and gave her a hug. "Of course dear, now I have to get these kids off to school and you have a new client downtown."

"This will be fun after a night of zero sleep." Shelley said.

"Remember your father's favorite saying dear, 'if you fly with the eagles'..." Janet turned to straighten Mark's shirt, blocking his view; he seemed curious to see what they were working on.

"Yes, I know." Shelley turned off the computer screen before Mark could read it. Dad's words were fun to recall and no matter how corny, she hoped his voice would never fade.

The next day, Mark and Jason found 'cool' sneakers within their first hour of shopping; any longer and the kids might have been driving Shelley home as she'd 'hit the wall' by 3pm, her energy gone, she could barely go another step. They arrived home by six and the kids jumped out of the car with their book bags and new shoes. Her legs ached, her briefcase was full of signed contracts and plans, and she needed a hot shower and downtime.

Janet met them at the front door, a veritable rock in the stream as they flowed past her on their way in; "Hi Grams."

"Guess what I found today." Janet said after the boys passed.

"Hi Mom; nice seeing you too." Shelley joked as she walked in to unload and called to the boys. "Take those shoes upstairs and don't damage the boxes; if we have to return them for any reason, we'll need them."

They rushed upstairs, and she turned to Janet. "Okay, what did you find today?"

"I found a genealogy line on William Christian Wodehause, Grandpa Edward's brother." There was a triumphant expression on Janet's face.

"Mom, that's wonderful. How did you do it?"

"Well, the great thing with older families is that someone has usually done the research, especially in the United Kingdom. One can query, follow a few leads and voila! The present name Wodehouse was Wodehause in the 18th century."

"Show me? I can't spend a lot of time, but I'd like to see what you've found."

In the den, Janet reopened the URL. "Here they are; William and his wife Rihanna, their sons and daughters."

"You're amazing Mom. Can you please print this for me to read later? Our new clients signed on for a $40K kitchen redo and I need to complete the drawings by Friday."

"Congratulations, that's wonderful, but don't you want to dig further on this?"

"I can't tonight Mom; feel free to dig; if you find anything on the estate— fantastic." She stopped to give Janet a hug. "Thanks for coming to my rescue again."

Shelley worked on kitchen designs that evening while Janet searched through the existing Wodehause files via an online genealogy site. Using an estimated date for William's arrival at Wodegate, and a range of five years, she found a reference to Edward. He and William may have been twins, both born in 1700.

Edward's son was unexpected; Shelley hadn't mentioned him. Brych Edward Wodehause was born in 1740 and by looking at nearby villages Janet found the boy at age nine registered for a Church of Scotland parish school.

She thought for a moment; by age 12 he'd be in secondary studies and at 17 or 18, in finals. If on to university, his graduation came around 1761; strange he wasn't heir to Wodegate by that time. "I wonder what happened." She pushed away from the desk.

Shelley was massaging her neck and reviewing her evening's work when Janet leaned around the corner. "May I interrupt for a few minutes?"

"I could use a break, how's the research?"

Janet laid her notes on the table. "These are the dates of early schooling for Edward's son Brych through what we know here as 'high school'. I'm wondering if he ever returned to the estate."

Shelley's eyes widened. "Edward had a son; why hasn't he mentioned him? It's clear he did or Nicholas wouldn't be here – there, five years ago; you know what I mean. Maybe it's time to ask Edward."

"What do you mean?" Janet said.

"Come to my room after the boys go to bed; if Edward responds, we'll ask him our questions." Shelley thought of something else. "He doesn't stay more than a few minutes so make notes of everything you need to ask."

"Yes... good idea, dear." Janet wasted no time in returning to her laptop and muffled a nervous laugh. I'm going to meet a ghost. After hearing his deep voice last night, she could hardly wait to see him. I'll never be able to speak of it to anyone she thought, but this is so exciting.

The kids clattered down the staircase to the kitchen. "Hi Grams," Jason said.

"Whatcha smiling about?" Mark said.

"Oh, nothing dear." Janet said. "Wash your hands and I'll get you both a snack."

By eleven o'clock, both boys were sound asleep, but Janet and Shelley decided it would be safer to talk to Edward downstairs in Janet's home office behind the kitchen.

"How do we call him?" Janet was nervous and drummed a pencil on the edge of the desk.

"Mom." Shelley took the pencil away. "You have the list?"

"Yes, dear, right here. Sorry about the noise."

"It's ok; we'll just sit here." She turned off the ceiling light and clicked on the desk lamp. "I don't know if strong light makes a difference or not. Edward instructed me to clear my mind and he will come." She closed her eyes and blocked out everything while Janet closed her eyes and sat without speaking. Moments passed in the dim light, but nothing happened.

Janet peeked from one eye. "Is he coming?"

"Noo juist haud on lassie, tisn't a street car tween here and the edge of haven." Edward said as he stood in front of them straight and proud in his uniform.

Janet's mouth fell open, but she remembered to shut it again.

Shelley pulled herself together and apologized. "Sorry, Edward this is my mother, Janet Lindquist. Mother, this is Edward Nicholas Wodehause."

"My honor mum." He nodded to Janet with a slight bow then turned to Shelley. "What dae ye need lass?"

"We have questions for you."

"Aboot?" He said.

"Aboot... about your son, Brych." Shelley found it hard not to echo his thick brogue and signaled to Janet to present her list.

"Mr. Wodehause..." Janet begins.

"Please, call me Edward mum, noo need ta formality."

"Thank you, Edward. We found information on Brych as he attended a parish school and university in Glasgow. How did your brother continue to hold the estate when Brych was of age?"

"Willum niver recognized Brych or acknowledged him ta the courts; he refused ta gi up his place as Trustee o the estate. Brych dae guid efter University, but didna hae the finances ta fight Willum. When he fand Carina, he wis happy withoot the responsality an estate would bring him."

"Carina was his wife." Shelley confirmed.

"Och aye, and a bonny yin that. Wi Christian Edward's birth, there wis no happier merit pair then they."

Janet regained her composure. "So no legal attempt was made to correct the wrong your brother perpetrated against you?"

"Nae mum." Edward said.

Shelley thought of something still unanswered. "Edward, do you know where your body was placed?"

"Ay, on a ben, the muntain looking oot ta Wodegate; twas planned wi a freend afore..." He looked away for a moment. "Twas sortit with Brych so A could look upon ma bonnie home. Willum and his lot knew nocht o it."

"Is the place marked?" Shelley said.

"Ay, by a large boulder standin on the ben; tis carved wi a Scottish burr ta its face and below it ma earthly remains lay. What more dae ye need fer I must awa aff."

"Who was your solicitor for the Will and Trust documents?" Janet said.

"A local man, A saw him only ance ta sign the papers, his name hae left me noo..."

"Do you remember what year it was?" Shelley said.

"Ah dinnae ken the year... left for Greenock and North America in 76. Sorry lasses ah must be farin."

Shelley rushed with one more question. "Will I be able to go back with the information we need?"

"Afore January it must be; call and ye'll see me." He disappeared as his last word lingered in the room.

"Wow." Janet said with trembling lip. "Edward knows how to make an exit."

Shelley stood up, her arms wrapped around herself. "Yes, he does."

CHAPTER Seven - Search

The next morning, Edward's words echoed in Shelley's mind while she waited for Janet in their home office; pressure was building in her now, so much to cover in only weeks.

Janet brought two cups of coffee. "You're up bright and early; I'm all yours, dear." Taking a sip, she picked up her pencil. "Where shall we start?"

"Local courts would have recorded William's claim on Wodegate. We need to confirm what county the estate is in and whether it's changed since 1776."

Janet added it to her list. "I'll find the nearest jurisdiction for that period and see if their archives are available online. Isn't Nicholas a solicitor? He knows more info on the justice system in Scotland than we ever will."

Shelley reminded her, "He's in a different place and time."

"He met you in 2011 and he'll remember you now." Janet said. "The documents haven't changed for Edward or William since 1776. Try finding Nicholas' phone number and call him; what can you lose?"

"It sounds wacky, but plausible... I guess. We can speculate he moved out of Wodegate." Shelley looked at her watch. "It's 12 noon in Scotland; give me a minute and I'll search for him." A few minutes later she'd found nothing.

"What about querying his old law practice?" Janet suggested. "He may be there again."

"Good idea." Shelley went back to her work. "Here, an article in an Aberdeen newspaper; 'Nicholas Wodehouse, solicitor with Berstyn Law Associates announced today he is moving to a new office in Glasgow, effective March 31st, 2013.' It doesn't give much detail; just that he sold his practice to an associate. I'll try to get a message to him through the old office." She found the business number in Aberdeen and put in the call.

"Berstyn Law, may I help you."

"Yes, I'd like to get a message to Nicholas Wodehouse please."

Shelley heard the woman pause. "Mr. Wodehouse is no longer here."

"Yes, I'm aware of that, but this is important. Might you get a message to him with my current name and number?"

"Well, I'm not supposed to, but give me the information and I'll try."

"Thank you for that." Shelley said. "This call is on behalf of his grandfather, Edward." Shelley rolled her eyes at Janet. After supplying her cell phone number and another round of thanks, she ended the call. "Thought I'd have a better chance on behalf of a family member."

Janet laughed; "Even if he's been dead for centuries." Then she looked around and added, "Sorry Edward, no disrespect intended."

Shelley smiled at her mother's remark. "Edward understands, desperate times and all that. Odd hearing someone say Nicholas' name five years later since seeing him... a few days ago."

"Even stranger hearing you say it, dear." Janet knew there was something between this Nicholas and her daughter though Shelley still couldn't admit to it. "Let's take a walk outside, we could use the fresh air and refocus."

Shelley exhaled. "You're right; I'll take my cell, just in case."

Outside, the fall leaves were in their orange phase and the yellow maples were shedding. She kicked through them on the garden walk as old habits made her pick up the near-perfect ones for pressing. A random fact popped into her mind as she held a leaf up to the sun; Wodegate's forests are already bare. The Scot days she'd buried, had found their way to the surface; Wodegate Castle, Jakke's sloppy licks of affection and just a smidgeon of Nicholas' hazel-green eyes were front and center for her now.

The cell interrupted her, and she pulled it from her pocket. "Hello, Shelley Lindquist."

"Shelley?"

"Yes... Nicholas?" There was silence, and she feared the connection was broken.

Then he spoke again. "I'm here. Where are you... how are you?"

Shelley chose a light-hearted reply. "Alive, well, and back from seeing you three days ago."

"It's been five years since you left, Shelley... I moved off the estate in 2012." His voice was different; quieter, more restrained with none of its usual 'snap'.

"I suspected that and looked up the estate yesterday on the internet. Edward tells me I have seven weeks to finish the research; my mother, Janet is handling that and he'll take me back with our findings."

"You're going back? But it's done... you're too late Shelley. I haven't heard Edward's voice since you left."

"It isn't too late." Shelley protested. "Edward appeared to us last night; I believe we can still change your future." Janet turned to walk back into the house.

"You weren't here Shelley." Nicholas said. "It was hell to pack up and move from Wodegate; I won't go through that again on a chance it'll be different next time... I can't." She listened to traffic noise in the background during his silence.

"Just promise you'll think on it." She said. "Call me back at this number after you do. We're continuing the search and could use your help." It was too hard to talk, and she took a deep breath to ease the tightness in her chest.

"Goodbye Shelley." Nicholas ended the connection and her countenance fell. What happened to him since she'd left?

Janet stood at the window watching as Shelley walked back. One look told her what she needed to know, and she met her daughter at the door for a hug. "It didn't sound good."

Her mother's instincts were on spot and Shelley accepted the hug, feeling safe in her arms. "He sounds sullen and beaten, not the Nicholas I knew in 2011."

"Did you save his number? Maybe you can call him back later today... " Janet suggested.

"Yes, I have it, but I won't beg him to save what's his. The effort has to be his; we can't do it for him." Shelley stepped out of her mother's arms.

Janet sensed her disappointment. "When did my daughter get so smart?"

"My last dose of 'smart' came when my ex walked away; I've become good at distancing myself when I'm not wanted." Shelley started back to her computer. "And I'm good at redirecting anger, so it's back to work on my client's kitchen. I'll forget castles, stubborn men and genealogy, for at least a day."

"Attah - girl" Janet encouraged. "Don't let em get to you."

The next day Janet sat at her computer with smug satisfaction; she'd contacted a registered genealogist in Scotland, a Jessica Davies, and arranged for her to delve into William Wodehause's family line. The money Janet's husband James left came handy and she knew he'd be alright with it; he was an adventurer and nothing ever scared him. Faith in God and James' example had kept her going through many trials over the years. Did she ever think she'd believe in ghosts and such? No, never, but she was confident that God could get creative and Edward's appearance was a miracle of sorts for both his grandson Nicholas, and for Shelley.

Shelley and the boys had left for the park, and the house was quiet which gave Janet time to think. Nicholas was a man she had yet to meet, but her daughter saw something in him despite his stubbornness. Nicholas told Shelley that Edward was silent with him since she left the estate and Janet wondered why; could Nicholas' closed mind block his grandfather from contacting him?

Janet's eyes brightened with an idea; Edward talked to her the other night, she wondered if he'd talk to her again.

Upstairs, she drew the curtains in her room and leaned back in her rocker. Clearing her mind as Shelley had instructed, she thought of Edward, that grand, proud man.

"Ay mum, are ye well?" Edward was again before her.

"Goodness. Thank you for coming and yes, I am well. I... a... called, because we have a problem and maybe the two of us can solve it."

A few days later, Janet received a phone call from Scotland. "Hello Mrs. Lindquist, Jessica Davies here, is this a good time to talk?"

"Yes, it's perfect. Please, call me Janet... and tell me you have news."

"Well, yes and no. William's full line is available; his sons first to last are documented, with Michale, born in 1901. Michale and his family immigrated to Canada and lived in Toronto, but after that, they drop off the grid."

"I'll search from this side, Jess; what of Wodegate Castle, any news there?"

"Inquiries are filed for any recorded Wills, but it's a slow process; don't give up, I'll keep at it." Jessica said. "A copy of William's line is coming to you on email and a certified hard copy will be sent; anything else before we ring off?"

Janet cleared her throat. "Can you suggest a way to find the latest rulings on Wodegate Castle Estate?"

Jessica considered the question for a moment. "Should be on public record; when did the court action take place?"

"We think after January 2012 with Wilson Bailey; we don't know if Nicholas Wodehouse or an unknown buyer were involved. Mr. Bailey lives in Glasgow and is in the steel mill business."

"His name sounds familiar; I've run across it somewhere, let me see what I can do. That's it so far and we'll keep in touch online unless we need to speak in person. Thank you for your generous retainer Janet, we're in good stead."

"Thank you, Jessica. You've done wonders in a short time." Janet put the phone down and clasped her hands. "I should've brought in an expert at the beginning."

Later that evening, Janet and Shelley discussed what they knew so far.

"Maybe we've missed the obvious." Shelley said. "Have you queried Arden Ross, Edward's friend and estate caretaker?"

"No, why?" Janet asked.

"He had a copy of the Will that Edward gave him." Shelley pulled a stool up to the breakfast counter. "Would Arden hide it in a common place on the estate, risking its ruin by vermin or fire in those days? He may have known ahead of time William and his family were planning to claim the estate; what if he took the papers with him off the estate?

"It's possible," Janet said. "But that leaves us with an endless number of options."

"Yes, but we could narrow the search by finding Arden after he left; chances are he worked for a living at something he knew how to do, forestry, game keeping, and horse breeding. Think of his jobs on the estate and find where he lived by census, church records and military files. Did he marry? Have kids?"

"Ok, ok, I get the picture and your idea inspires more of my own. There's something I have to confess." Janet said. "I've hired a genealogist in Scotland, her name is Jessica Davies and she's already made progress."

"Mom, that has to be expensive."

Janet smiled patiently. "True, but it's within reason for what's at stake here. Your dad left extra 'mad' money for me, and I want to do this."

Shelley knew she couldn't argue with her once a decision was made. "Then thank you Mom, I mean it. What has this Jessica done so far?"

"I've left everything she's sent on my desk and expect more by overnight delivery, so take a look when you can. Now, what would you like for breakfast?"

Several days later, a package arrived from Great Britain; Janet signed for it, waved the deliveryman off and carried it to the kitchen island where there was plenty of room to spread out its contents.

A multi-paged contract for Wodegate was on top and she leafed through it then marveled at one detail. "So Mr. Bailey didn't buy the estate, he inherited a Leasehold from his grandfather. I wonder if Nicholas knows this."

A copy of an Ottawa, Ontario newspaper article came next; 'Michale Wodehause Dies' the 1924 article read. 'Wife and child killed as auto turns over.' It was heartbreaking to read, even though it happened over ninety years ago. Janet paused for a moment, thankful for her own family's wellbeing before reading a note from Jessica.

Dear Janet,

Hope these documents are useful, I continue to search for any information on the missing Will for Edward.

I have a copy of Arden Ross's death record in 1810; his family consisted of two sons and a wife so I'm examining church records for christenings, marriages, etc. I hope to have a sheet soon on descended relatives who may still exist. The good news is, several Ross families live in Scotland and have documented their family trees.

I'm hustling to find as much as possible before the November deadline. It's a privilege to be involved and I have the time to dedicate. I will call if any further from you is needed.

Best Regards, Jessica Davies

Shelley read through the documents later that evening. "Jess sounds encouraged and I feel less stressed. Glad one of us is thinking straight and hired an expert. The Leasehold means a reprieve for Nicholas while we find new evidence for the Court, if he's going to Court." She added with some doubt and a weary sigh as she stared out the window for a moment.

Janet studied her daughter's face. "You look tired, tough day?"

"It's been busy. We have the kitchen in full redo and it's going well. I'm rounding up final tile and flooring choices for the customer. This is busy season before the holidays, and inventories are limited, but we'll get it together."

"I know you will dear. What would you like for supper?"

"Don't worry about me, I'm not that hungry. I'll forage in the fridge."

"You're sure? Alright then, the kids have eaten so I'll just get them pointed toward the shower and ready for school tomorrow."

Janet took to the stairs, and hummed as she did. Each day they made progress and since speaking with Edward and Jessica, she had more hope than ever.

Nicholas never called Shelley back; without him, there was nothing anyone could do even as Jessica found further information. He was the heir; the only one who could take legal action to reclaim his rightful estate. It'd been weeks since they talked and each day increased the odds against his change of heart. Shelley secretly felt her life was again taking a dismal turn.

November arrived and her work projects done, Shelley's schedule was cleared for home and family during the holidays. Being on pause for Edward and Jessica had complicated the season and her optimism was growing harder to prolong. She'd grown very serious about her promise to Edward and planned to return to 2011 Scotland in December with the needed proof for Nicholas. Now, only three weeks were left before time ran out and it all became a wasted plan.

CHAPTER Eight - Plans

"Nicolas lad."

A voice he hadn't heard in five years called him one evening as he sat at his desk. He was glad to hear his grandfather's voice and had missed him, but he hesitated to reply and tried to think of reasons for this sudden contact.

Then for the first time in their strange relationship, Edward appeared in front of him. The sight of him in full highlander military dress was a jolt, but impressive and he felt the man... ghost before him deserved his respect.

"Good evening Grandfather."

"How are ye?" Edward said.

"I've no answer for that... but it's good to see you."

Edward sensed the toll taken on his grandson during the last few years; the light graying at his temples, his voice changed and quieter since he last visited him.

"Ye once told me ye'd no hae me in yer love life, lad."

"Yes, I said those words didn't I; no need to worry now, I've driven her away and lost Wodegate to Wilson Bailey." Nicholas closed up the papers on his desk. "What can I do for you Grandfather?"

"It's Shelley, her mither Janet, and her lads, Mark and Jason." Edward watched for his reaction which came immediately.

"Is she okay... are they alright?" Nicholas asked.

"A've niver seen a lass so low; Shelley's noo happy and waits these remaining three weeks fer word on ma Will; Ah tak full responsibeelity fer puttin her in tha position. More important, she's bidin fer ye and admits ye misst ane subject at Wodegate."

"What subject?" Nicholas said.

"The ane thing in life tha shoud niver be unspoken, lad, love." Edward wondered how he'd take his meddling, but his grandson remained silent and sat looking at him. "Ye have nane to say... wi whit's at stake?"

"What can I say Grandfather? When she called to ask for my help, I knew I couldn't succeed in regaining Wodegate... or her and threw away my second chance without a word. I've nothing to offer; it's five years since we met and thousands of miles between us; she has a family of her own and the estate remains in Bailey's hands."

"Hae ye ever thought there micht be a wey to work it oot wi Bailey?" Edward said.

"What do you mean? I don't have enough money to buy back the estate or invest in its renovation."

"Wilson Bailey hae a Leasehold inherited from his grandfaither, not ownership o'the estate; ye hae time Nicholas." Edward said. "The Court, it wad accept proof o ma death efter the war tae prescrive on Willum's treachery.

"The answer is ta find Arden Ross's family; Shelley's mum hired a helper ta do that, an A'v a suggestion... should ye hae the gurr."

"What is it Grandfather?" Nicholas' interest revived.

"Find ma body; the papers micht be hidden thare by Brych and Arden."

"That's crazy! You can't just dig up bodies in this century. This isn't primitive Scotland, Grandfather, we have laws now. Besides, I have no way of knowing where you... your earthly remains are." Nicholas realized his words might bring sadness to Edward and didn't mean to sound unfeeling. "I'm sorry to speak so. The truth is I'm glad you're here, you're the only family I've ever had who truly cares."

"Ah lad, it means much to hear ye say it. Noo first, contact Shelley and Janet, they hae more information on the Wodehause family. Put yer heids thegither; if anyone can, ye'll figure oot a plan ta revisit Wodegate and work it oot wi Bailey. I kenna stay eny longer the nicht, but ken I'll be watchin ye."

Nicholas paced the study after Edward left. To try again for Wodegate would take everything he could muster; as for Shelley, he didn't feel worthy. And what did Edward mean 'work it out with Bailey'?

Janet shooed the boys out the door to get them to school early so she could spend the day in the library and visit her lawyer friend with the Leasehold document. "Don't expect me before dinner tonight, dear."

"Bye guys." Shelley watched as they stuffed themselves into the car.

The quiet in the house was deafening after the morning's get-ready-for-school din. The breakfast dishes needed a wash-up and her second cup of coffee was due. Still in her pajamas and hair a mess, the empty house offered a rare 'alone' day for her. Maybe I'll just stay in pajamas until three and change before everyone comes home she thought. What freedom!

After the dishes were up to dry, she refilled her cup and sat on the couch to browse through the files from Jessica. The doorbell startled her and broke her concentration, but she managed to put her cup down without spilling it.

When she opened the door, a man wearing sunglasses with a carryon bag in his hand suddenly smiled at her; her mind went blank and words failed.

Nicholas waited then finally asked, "May I come in?"

"Yes... I think... please, come in." She managed to get her words out and stepped back from the doorway.

He placed his suitcase inside the door and removed his sunglasses then glanced at her pajamas and messy hair. "I should have called."

"What and ruin the element of surprise?" Shelley said and ran a hand through the top of her pillow hair. "What are you doing here? The last I heard, you were done with Wodegate."

"I was."

Shelley realized they were still in the hallway. "Would you like some breakfast or coffee?"

"Coffee, please; they fed us on the plane, if you can call a box of sandwiches and a cookie, food." He hung his jacket on the coat rack before following her to the kitchen. "You have a beautiful home, Shelley."

"Thank you. Not what you're used to, I guess." She said as she poured two cups of coffee at the breakfast bar.

"What do you mean?" Then he noticed her crooked smile. "You're testing me again aren't you? I haven't lived in a castle for years. My home is an apartment in Glasgow, a one bedroom with a view of the river where I often walk to destress after work. This coffee's excellent, by the way."

"Mom makes it; don't ask me what she does, but mine is never the same." Shelley waited to see what he'd say next, it was his turn. When he remained silent, she tried again. "Nicholas...," At the same time he said, "Shelley..."

He started again. "We're not good at small talk, are we. Shelly, I came to offer you my apologies."

"For what?" Shelley could think of plenty but wanted to hear him say it.

"For being a stubborn, conceited idiot while you were at Wodegate and for failing you when you called me for help. You were coming to my rescue, but I was so full of self-pity, I couldn't see it. Can you forgive me?" He fixed her in a serious stare, "I truly want to work this out with you."

What he'd just asked of her wasn't easy after their last phone conversation that kept replaying in her mind. Though he was handsome, even in washed-out jeans, t-shirt, and unkempt dark hair, he couldn't reconcile his past behavior with a few words.

"Why the change of heart?" She said.

"Edward visited yesterday evening, appearing to me for the first time. We came to a mutual agreement, that I needed to see you and clear up our relationship."

"You think we have a problem, do you?" Shelley played dumb just to aggravate him.

"Not anymore. I own it now and take full responsibility. Most of my young life was spent away from family in boarding school; it's not an excuse, just a fact. That type of upbringing breeds a self-contained man who thinks he needs no one and has little tolerance for those who do. It's hard to change what's been drilled into one since childhood, but I finally recognize I do need people in my life, especially you."

She saw something new in his eyes since they'd last met and arose from her seat, though it was difficult. "I need to get dressed, you interrupted my free day." He looked askance and she explained.

"You know, a free-to-do-whatever-you-want day. Mom's at the library and the kids are in school; I don't look like this all the time." She waved her hand from head to toe as if a game show model showing off curtain number one and broke his serious mood.

He laughed and understood. "You look wonderful to me." But she gave him 'the look', knowing that no one would prefer her in her present state.

"Alright, truth is, I could use cleaning up too." He said and rose to his feet. "I'm wearing bits of my sandwich on the front of this shirt. Is there a second bath?"

Shelley showed him around the house to the guest bedroom. "Make yourself at home Nicholas. If you get hungry, feel free to venture into the kitchen."

In her room, her mind continued to whirl; his apology seemed sincere, but totally out of character for the man she'd known. Maybe he has changed in his five years since we met, but we have too much ground to cover by December and don't need distractions. Everything inside her said 'whoa girl', you've only known him a few weeks'.

Janet opened the front door and reached to hang her sweater on the coat rack. Whose is this she wondered as she examined a sports jacket then looked through to the kitchen where a strange man was examining the fridge's contents.

"Excuse me, may I help you?" She watched as the man stood up and bumped his head on the freezer door.

"Ow!" He turned around to face her, his hand holding the top of his head. "Hello, you must be Shelley's mother. I'm Nicholas Wodehouse." He came toward her with hand extended.

"Well, Nicholas, how nice to meet you. Are you alright?"

"Yes, I'm fine... hard head, no harm. Sorry for the cooler, but Shelley said to forage if I was hungry."

Janet saw his embarrassment. "No problem Nick; let me get started on dinner, I lost track of time at the library. When did you arrive?" He followed her back to the kitchen where she pulled potatoes, steaks, and salad fixings from the fridge.

"This morning, I took the red-eye." He felt the knot on his head and sat at the breakfast counter. "Shelley pointed me to the guest room, but I can get a hotel room for tonight with no problem."

"Nonsense Nick, the guest room is yours, if you want it. Besides, I assume you're here to work on your case for Wodegate?" Janet said.

"Yes... and to set things straight between Shelley and me."

"And have you?" Janet asked as she hesitated in her food prep.

He smiled and said "It's a start, so yes."

"Then the trip is a success Nick, don't you agree?"

"Yes, I hope so." He liked this woman, straight to the point with no hidden innuendoes.

Janet turned to her work again with a smile glued to her face; Edward had done a wonderful job and she resisted doing a victory dance around the kitchen for Nicholas' sake.

"It's good to see you here. I've been working with a genealogist, Jessica Davies in Scotland for your benefit.

She's made marvelous progress in finding information to help our... your fight for Wodegate."

"That's good news." Nicholas said. "I look forward to hearing all about it, but tonight will be a short evening for me; I've been awake too long at this point."

"Of course." She said. "Enjoy a good dinner then get your rest; plenty of time in the morning."

"May I help with something?" He asked.

"That would make this go quicker; can you wash these potatoes and wrap them in paper towels for the microwave?"

"Be glad to Mrs. Lindquist."

"Please, call me Janet. I know so much about you, I feel we're already good friends."

When Shelley entered, Janet and Nicholas were preparing food together and sharing a glass of wine. "I see she's making you work for your dinner."

"Yes, but I like being part of the kitchen help. I don't cook a lot at home; easier to go to a restaurant and avoid the dishes." Nicholas said.

"Well, dishes are part of the deal in this house. Though the boys take turns, homework sometimes takes precedence. Speaking of which, where are they, Mom?"

"They went to their friend Jamie's house; his parents are throwing him a slumber party for his birthday." Janet said. "I thought it would be alright since we know them and it's Friday."

"That's fine, they're great neighbors and close enough the boys can call us and walk home if they want." Shelley said.

"The boys are getting more independent, daughter. I think their days of staying close to home are rapidly ending; soon they'll be teenagers." Janet put out plates and silverware and they took their seats.

"You're right, Mom, I do get a tad over-protective; habit I guess, but I'll work on it." She turned to Nicholas, "Do you have everything you need in the guest room?"

"Yes, thank you; I brought my own toothbrush."

"Ha ha." Shelley joked.

"I walked out into your backyard earlier, it's warmer here than at home and very pleasant." He took a bite of steak. "Mmm, my compliments to the chef, Janet."

"We do have snow in the winter." Shelley said. "But it never stays long. I enjoy our 'chilly' days and the flowers in spring, but don't look forward to summer's humidity."

"Scotland has its ups and downs as well; lots of rain, plenty of time to read and sit at the fireside." Nicholas said. "You learn to get on with whatever no matter the weather."

"I remember the pile of wellies in the kitchen at Wodegate; there was a pair in every size." Shelley said.

"We're never without them to tramp the countryside." A yawn caught him unawares. "Excuse me; the time difference has me in its grip."

"Why don't you turn in early?" Janet said. "Shelley and I can handle this."

"I'm sorry to duck out, but think I'll have to if I'm to be in any shape for the morning. Good night, thank you for a delicious dinner, see you both in the morning."

When he'd reached the guest room, and they heard the door shut, Janet turned to Shelley. "Well, daughter, what do you think?"

"Ok, Mom, I know you won't stop until I tell you; he apologized and I want to believe he's trying to change." Shelley carried their dishes to the dishwasher.

"That's wonderful dear, I'm happy for you; now that Nicholas is here, we can get busy. Let's meet in the morning and share everything we've learned so far; three heads are better than two. And on that note, I'm turning in early; love you dear."

Shelley smiled at her. "You too, Mom."

CHAPTER Nine - Question

Things that interrupt sleep started to happen around eight a.m. in the Lindquist household.

First, the kids arrived home and let themselves in with the key hidden for them when they forgot their own. Nicholas' jacket still hung on the hall tree and Jason spied it.

"Whose is this?"

Mark shrugged his shoulders and headed upstairs for his bed; Jason and his friend Jamie were up most of the night watching stupid stuff on the computer which kept him awake, too.

"Don't you want to know?" Jason started towards the guest room figuring it might yield answers. "Follow me." He motioned to Mark who rolled his eyes, but followed.

They carefully opened the door and spied Nicholas among the sheets, but Jason decided to tiptoe in for a closer look and satisfy his curiosity.

"Jason, get back here." Mark said in a whisper. So intent was Jason on seeing Nicholas' face, he didn't see the stray shoe on the floor and fell over it, straight across the foot of the bed. Nicholas sat up from sound sleep directly in front of the startled Jason and they locked eyes before Jason jumped off the bed and ran out. Mark had already vacated the hallway and was in his bed by the time Jason slammed their bedroom door in haste.

Janet and Shelley, now fully awake, opened their bedroom doors and with knowing looks, turned to the boys' room. It was clear both kids had something to hide; Mark was awake in his bed and Jason sat on his.

"Well, which one of you wants to begin?" Shelley said while Janet turned to start breakfast downstairs.

"Begin what Mom?" Jason said.

"Please get on with it." She responded.

Jason squirmed then gave her the story on their downstairs event.

"Really! You both know better than to go into someone's private space, including the guest room when a guest is inside. I expect you both to be dressed and downstairs in five minutes; you'll apologize to Mr. Wodehouse as soon as he appears. You couldn't wait to meet him, so now you will." With her last word she stalked from the room and closed the door behind her.

Jason looked at his brother. "Wow, she was mad."

"Don't look at me; I just wanted to get some sleep." Mark said and pulled himself out of bed. "Thanks to you, that's not happening."

When Shelley came into the kitchen, Janet and Nicholas sat at the breakfast bar drinking coffee.

"I'm so sorry Nicholas; Jason is the incurable of the two. Once his imagination flairs it runs wild, he follows it wherever it leads... even into the guest room where a guest is sleeping."

Nicholas laughed. "Don't worry; as soon as I sat up, they both disappeared out the door. Jason fell over one of my shoes onto the bed or I wouldn't have heard them at all."

"There's no excuse and I've told them they both need to apologize." Shelley said. "So play the part of one wronged until they do, okay?"

"If that's what you recommend." He winked at Janet and returned to his coffee.

Within a few minutes, both kids came to the kitchen. Their steps faltered when they saw Nicholas, but there was no escape and they took their seats.

"Boys, this is Mr. Nicholas Wodehouse from Scotland. These are my sons, Mark and Jason."

"Good morning, sir, I'm Mark." Nicholas nodded and shook his hand across the counter.

Jason followed his brother's example; "Good morning, I'm Jason, how are you?"

"A little less sleep than I'd planned on, but I'm good." Nicholas shook his hand.

"Yeh, about that," Jason said. "I'm sorry I woke you up; I just wanted to see who was here."

Mark took over after his brother's slack excuse. "Yes, I'd like to add my apologies, as well. Please forgive us, it won't happen again." Jason looked at him sideways then back to his mother.

"Okay boys, no problem and I trust it won't." Nicholas told them. "How was the party last night?"

"It was fun and the food was great." Mark answered. "Jason stayed up the longest."

"I see, so you had more sleep?"

"Not exactly; Jason and Jamie were laughing too loud." Mark said.

"Oh, what were you laughing at, Jason?" Shelley asked.

"Nothing, we were just watching stuff on Jamie's computer; kids falling off bikes, cracking up on their skate boards, funny stuff."

"I don't think it's humorous when people get hurt and I hope you realize that someday. You're both grounded for your little invasion of privacy this morning, so go to your room and don't come out until dinnertime, understand?"

"Why Mom, I didn't do anything." Mark said.

"Jason is your brother and you shouldn't have allowed him to enter Mr. Wodehouse' room, now go." The boys left the kitchen with chins on their chests.

"I feel bad they're in trouble because of me." Nicholas said.

"Because of you?" Janet said. "They were on their own and it's never too early to teach someone good manners and the rules of society. We still love them and the sun will rise tomorrow. Now, who's hungry; omelets all around? And yes, I'll take breakfast up to the boys." She said before Nicholas could ask.

After breakfast, they sat at the dining room table to discuss what Jessica had sent. "Now that you know Wilson Bailey doesn't own Wodegate; how does it affect your drive to recover it?" Janet asked.

Nicholas frowned. "On the one hand, I'm encouraged, but also a little frightened. I've saved a nice sum from my legal practice over the last few years, but doubt it's enough to put Wodegate back on its feet again or keep up with expenses until it is.

"There's opportunity for timber revenue, and tourist bookings for seasonal fishing and hunting, but it'll take time to build that up; meanwhile, monthly bills will keep coming."

"Why not find a partner, Nicholas?" Shelley said. "A person who'd invest funds in return for a percentage of the estate's profit, beginning in say, five years?"

"It should be someone who appreciates the place as you do and whom you can trust." Janet said.

"That's a large order." Nicholas said. "Right now, the only one I can think of that fits the description, haunts us." He drew a smile from the girls.

"You're right..." Janet said. "Edward would make a great partner, but he has 'higher obligations'. This may sound just as unlikely, but what of Wilson Bailey?"

"Does he care for Wodegate or just the money it might bring him?" Shelley said.

"We've had conversations in the past; he respects the estate, but his mind is on steel." Nicholas said. "His dream is to one day go big with his grandfather's old mill.

"Steel hasn't done well in Scotland for years." Nicholas continued. "After the Prime Minister privatized the industry in 1988, things started downhill, a disaster for West-Central Scotland which led the industry for years. I question whether a small mill could keep up on its own with the current technology and money larger corporations have to invest. Wilson may be blinded by respect for his grandfather."

"Does he realize you two are related, Nicholas?" Janet said.

"How are we related? This is the first I've heard of it."

"Per Jessica Davies, Wilson's distant grandfather John Benjamin Bailey II, was the son of Ann Bailey Wodehause's brother." Janet said. "You two are seventh-removed cousins."

"I'm amazed; it could change things I suppose." Nicholas said. "Do you think Wilson's aware of it? He may have more than financial interest in the place."

Shelly leaned forward. "I think there's a good chance he doesn't know; how many of us have gone back seven generations into our family's history? Heck, most people don't have a clue about their great grandparents."

"Jessica's info may improve his thoughts for the estate once he's informed." Janet said.

"I don't want to count on that." Nicholas said.

"It's certainly worth knowing if you decide to consider a partner." Janet said. "On another note, Jessica's been looking for relatives of Edward's friend, Arden Ross; there's a chance the Will could have passed to future generations via his family."

"It seems impossible that a two-hundred year old document could survive with ordinary care that long." Nicholas said.

"True, but there's always an exception and we can't afford to leave any stone unturned." Shelley said.

"Funny you should put it that way... well, not 'funny' per se." Nicholas said. "When Edward came to see me last week, he suggested I exhume his body; I refused."

"Whatever for? Shelley asked. "Doesn't it require a permit or something?"

"Yes, but he didn't put it that way and used the words 'dig up my remains'. He thinks there's a chance Edward's son Brych and Mr. Ross put the Will and Trust papers in the grave with him." Nicholas said. "I don't even know where he's buried, but assume he lies somewhere in an ancient graveyard around Glasgow."

All went quiet for a few minutes then Janet cleared her throat. "We know where he is because we asked during one of his visits. He says Arden and Bryce put him somewhere near Wodegate on a hill."

"Not exactly a map-worthy description, is it?" Nicholas said. "I don't know if I could do the deed and strongly hope we find our proof elsewhere."

By the end of the morning they agreed Nicholas, not Shelley, should be the one to travel back in time to 2011 with Edward and meet Wilson Bailey in court.

"I agree." Nicholas said. "I missed Wilson's last appearance and completely misconstrued what his legal rights were for Wodegate."

Later, Shelley and Nicholas took a walk in the neighborhood after dinner. The night air was warm, the mosquitos "not too bad, if we keep moving." Shelley said. "Speaking of moving, how do you feel about traveling back in time?"

"A little scary, but I want to do it, no matter." He said. "What does it feel like?"

"It was like traveling on a blue light and suddenly dropped onto a foreign planet. The actual trip isn't bad, you'll be disoriented at first, but it soon passes. I knew what to expect the second time, definitely easier without panic." She laughed about it now, but couldn't when it first happened.

"I'll do it for grandfather." Nicholas said. "He deserves to see the true story brought forward and history updated with William's betrayal of his own brother and nephew. The name of Wodehause should stay connected to its ancestral seat, with or without me in residence."

"I can understand you wanting the truth to be revealed." Shelley stopped walking. "What if the Court doesn't see it that way; will you be able to walk away at that point?"

"It's become secondary to me now, Shelley." Nicholas said. "I can face any outcome of the Court as long as our family's history is corrected and won't relinquish that."

"I believe you'll succeed, I don't know if it will be the way you envision, but I'm rooting for you." She said.

"Good, because I want you to come back to Scotland with me this week, and help search for Edward's final resting place; I've decided it's too great an opportunity to let pass. You notice things I don't and it would be a tremendous help to have you there; please say yes, Shelly."

She could tell by his voice he was completely serious, but couldn't go back to Scotland again... could she? "I need to think about it tonight."

"I realize your obligations here." He said. "I know it won't be as easy for you as for me. You've never accepted my apology; does this mean you don't?"

"There are many things to consider before I drop my family life in the middle of the holidays and run off to Scotland." She knew she could have put it better as soon as the words escaped. Nicholas looked as if he'd been struck.

"Please Nicholas; that was unintentionally harsh." He started to turn away but she put her hand on his arm. "Just listen...please. You talked of old wounds that made you the way you are and I do accept your apology for that. What you don't know is that I have scars, too.

"Ten years ago my ex decided his job was more important than his family and left us to fend for ourselves. I understand scars because he left them on me and my ability to trust anyone again."

His heart melted when he heard her explanation. "It's okay Shelley, I do know your family is way more important than some dusty old archives from centuries ago and I understand even more now. You're a very lucky woman to have what you have here; don't ever take it lightly."

"I'll give you my decision in the morning." She said.

Shelley weighed Nicholas' words, pro and con as she lay in bed that night. It's all about him isn't it she thought. He's carried heavy responsibility all his life and couldn't be blamed for needing moral support, but he thinks I can leave just like that; so typical of a self-centered man.

It'd been painful to acknowledge how her ex-husband's actions had affected her, especially to Nicholas. She'd resolved never to get involved with anyone remotely like him again and kept that promise for ten years. But she argued with herself now; 'this is aiding a friend' and finally fell asleep.

CHAPTER Ten – Going Back

Shelley woke abruptly to find Janet in her room. "Mom? What are you doing here, is everything alright?"

"Shhh, yes everything is fine." Janet whispered. "I thought this would be a good time to talk."

Shelley looked at the clock on her dresser. "Yes...three-thirty in the morning is terrific, if you're an owl. What's going on?"

"Edward visited me a little while ago." Janet said. "He tells me Nicholas asked you to come back to Scotland with him."

Shelley sat up and fluffed her hair. "So much for the morning's breaking news."

"Have you decided to go?"

"I decided last night to consider it." She said. "This is a big deal, Mom; I'd be leaving you-all over the holidays."

"And?" Janet prodded.

"And...I'd be alone with Nicholas in Scotland...again. Am I being wise here? I've truly known him all of a few weeks and honestly, he reminds me of my ex, self-centered and stubborn. What do you think, Mom?"

"I think you should trust your instincts, but consider what your heart says, too. Remember, you have options this time and can always fly home, it's not like before. Besides, I like him and I've seen how happy he makes you by being here."

"Really? You saw that in a couple of days?" Shelley hung her legs over the edge of the bed and sat up. "It wasn't clear to me last night... but I'd like to go."

"Then I say 'Go' and don't worry about us. We'll miss you but we'll be fine." Janet smiled at her. "You need to tell the boys first thing so they can agree to let you go, know what I mean?"

Shelley did. "Yes, your reverse psychology methods are genius and pretty slick on me; hope they work as well on the boys."

"I've got your back, dear."

Shelley hugged her. "You always do."

Janet had a scrumptious breakfast ready by the time everyone came to the kitchen. The breakfast bar was laden with a platter of warm pancakes, sausage patties browned and crispy, biscuits and a server of hot gravy nearby. Sectioned oranges were piled into a bowl and her special coffee added its aroma to the house.

Nicholas smiled when he saw the feast she'd prepared. "Good morning, Janet; you heard the rooster this morning?"

She set the grill aside. "Something like that."

"Good morning Mr. Wodehouse." Mark and Jason said in unison.

"Eat up guys." Janet sat by Jason. "Let me know if you need more pancakes, I have em in the oven."

Shelley glanced at Nicholas. "Mark, Jason, Mom, I have something to discuss with you."

"What about?" Mark said, his mouth stuffed with pancake.

"Nicholas has asked me to come to Scotland for two weeks and help him find some legal papers." She saw Nicholas' head snap up and smiled at him.

"Are you coming back by Christmas?" Jason said.

"There's a possibility that I won't, but you should know I'll do everything I can to get back by then. You see Nicholas' 7th great-grandfather lived in a castle named Wodegate and it's still there. His grandfather went off to fight the War of Independence here in America and when he returned to Scotland, his brother had taken his home and wouldn't give it back."

"That was pretty stinky of him." Jason said.

"I agree, Jason." Nicholas smiled his approval of Jason's take on the matter.

"1776 was a long time ago." Mark spoke up. "What can you do about it now?"

"There are two things we must prove." Nicholas said. "First is the fact that grandfather did come back from the War alive and second, that his brother cheated him out of his property by lying to the Court."

Shelley added, "If we can find the records we need, Wodegate may be returned to Nicholas' grandfather and his family."

Mark summed it up. "I hope you have good luck Mr. Wodehouse. Mom always says what goes around, comes around and it sounds like your family didn't get what should have been theirs; now you have another chance."

Shelley was proud of Mark and took a deep breath before asking her question. "So, do both of you feel okay about my going with Nicholas?"

"Okay with me Mom." Mark said between bites.

"Jason, what do you think?" Her silent son still ate without comment.

He finally looked at her. "It's... okay, but try to get here for Christmas. If you don't, are you going to bring us presents from Scotland?"

Everyone burst into laughter. "Yes I will bring presents either way." She said and left her seat to give both boys a hug. "You guys are the best and I love you very much."

Nicholas felt a trace of melancholia as he watched them; he couldn't remember his parents ever talking with him the way Shelley did with her boys. "Thanks guys for letting your Mom go, and I promise to take good care of her."

The next day, Shelley and Nicholas caught their plane in Atlanta with barely enough time to sit down and buckle up. The flight over the Atlantic was a long eight hours, and they used the downtime to relax, talk and grab a few hours' sleep.

At Heathrow, they bought breakfast sandwiches to get them through after the sparse meal received on the way over then boarded a smaller plane for Glasgow.

It was raining in Glasgow at seven p.m. and Shelley was glad she'd stuffed her jacket into the outside pocket of her carryon. Nicholas left his car in airport parking, so they picked it up and were on their way in no time.

Both were beginning to flag by the time he parked at the apartment and Shelley was thankful for the elevator that carried them mercifully up to his fifth floor loft with no stairs to climb.

She was surprised by the place; it was a mosh of décor, modern and simple furniture in beige and wood tones, with some surprising elements. Classic art of the Scottish countryside hung on a few of the walls and several antiques from farm and early life in the 18th and 19th centuries were displayed. One small, framed piece caught her eye near the door and she stopped to look.

"Is this...?" She didn't finish because it sounded too sentimental for him.

"The primroses you picked when we rode up to the stream, remember?" He looked at the frame with her.

"I do remember, but I left them on the mantel before Edward brought me home, how did you find them?"

"I went to your room to tell you how much I wanted you to stay, but you'd already left. I looked around to see if you'd left a note and the flowers were in a cup on the mantel. I took them to the library and pressed them in paper between the pages of grandfather's Shakespeare tome; it seemed an appropriate place." He was shy about what he'd done and didn't meet her eyes. "The framer did a nice job didn't he?"

"A beautiful job." She turned away, uncomfortable at being so close to him. "I don't know about you, but I'm beat and really need to sleep. Where's my bunk?"

"I'll sleep on the sofa down here." Nicholas said. "You take the bed in the loft. I can sleep anywhere and a girl needs her space."

He insisted and Shelley was too tired to protest.

In the morning while Nicholas showered and dressed, Shelley phoned Janet.

"Mom, hi, we're here."

"Hello dear, glad you made it safely. What are you doing today?" Janet said.

"I'm not sure; we haven't had breakfast yet. Any news from Jessica?"

"No, but I sent a message to let her know you've arrived. You should get together when she's available; I believe she lives west of Edinburgh, not too far to meet in the middle."

"Good idea, are the boys okay?" Shelley missed them already.

"Of course; they went off to school in good time and I'm picking them up for McDonald's this afternoon. Don't worry; they'll be fine." Janet said.

"I know they will with you there. I'll let you know our plans by email to save on phone calls. Love you Mom, and give the boys a kiss for me."

"Love you too dear, be safe." Janet said.

Shelley stood at the window watching the morning traffic cross over the river Clyde as it ran through the city. She was eager to venture out into Scotland now that the rain had cleared.

Nicholas entered smelling of soap and aftershave. "Sightseeing from the window?"

"Yes, I guess I am, but I'd much rather be outside. Why don't we drive up to Wodegate while we have the good weather?" Shelley said.

"I suppose it would be wise; how soon can you be ready?"

"If you feed me along the way, I'm good to go right now." She said.

"Then let's get out there." They grabbed a change of clothes, a few munchies, and bottled water and were out the door in ten minutes.

After a quick stop for some breakfast sandwiches, Nicholas took the main road north out of Glasgow and within the hour, Shelley was lost; even her phone didn't have connection in the low-lying mountains.

"I'm glad you know where you're going, I'd have to call Police Scotland to rescue me." She said.

He laughed at her. "Have a little faith; we're headed generally north with leeway for the hills and have about thirty minutes to go before we take the long drive west from the main road to the estate. It's a one lane track, and you might see some wild life – red deer abound up here."

"What are your expectations at the estate?" Shelley said.

"I'm curious about its condition. I know Wilson had no plans to live there, but I hope he's at least kept up with the maintenance.

"I also want to take a look at the surrounding hillsides from the river. You said Edward described his resting place as 'overlooking' the estate." Nicholas held up some fancy glasses. "I brought binoculars."

After reaching the western cutoff, they drove over a rise lined by Norway spruce; Shelley saw through them to blue water in the valley below and strained forward for a better look. "What is that down there?"

"It's the river running to the Loch on its way to the coast; my ancestors initially came inland to the site of Wodegate by boat." Nicholas said.

"Beautiful scenery; now I'm sorry I didn't take you up on your offer to see the river." She met his eyes for a second.

"The river will always be here." He said. "We may have to meet it further down its course if our plan for the estate doesn't work out. I'll take you to it one way or another, I promise."

The castle's roofline appeared over the trees and Nicholas parked the car outside the old courtyard. He sat quietly looking at the place, his first glimpse since leaving for Aberdeen. Shelley stayed silent to give him the moment.

He noticed the grass was trimmed around walls and drive, and a planter of heather sat near the front steps. "It doesn't look too neglected; shall we knock on the door?"

"Why not." Shelley pushed out of the car and joined him to climb the stone stairway to the lion's head doors. Nicholas used one of the iron rings to knock and before long, the door swung open.

CHAPTER Eleven
Edward in His Time

1776 - 1782

*M*ajor Edward Nicholas Wodehause heeded the call to duty and joined Lord Howe's British Army, the 71st Highland Foot, in 1775. The Regiment sailed from Greenock Scotland and arrived in North America in July 1776. British troops, formed with German mercenaries, Irish and Scots, fought bravely in New York, Brandywine, and Wilmington for King George the 3rd then sailed south to Georgia.

After capture of Savannah and Augusta they continued to Charleston which surrendered in May 1780. The Regiment was joined by men from other companies and stayed in the area to help hold the lines in the southern campaign, but they were thin in number from their original force.

Supplies began to dwindle by 1781 and soon stopped. Britain was fighting multiple conflicts; the French not only sent financial support to the Americans, but secured Chesapeake Bay, Britain's primary route for reinforcements and supplies. It fell to the British troops in the South to 'requisition' their own supplies from locals and leave receipts for payment later when they could.

Edward led his men through several skirmishes with American troops during the British occupation; the colonists fought seemingly without planned movement, hiding in the swamps and woods by day and striking without notice in the night when an opportunity presented.

It was during one of these skirmishes that Edward sustained serious injury by an axe to his left leg leaving the bone shattered. His men carried him back to camp and he awoke to see Dr. Robert Jackson looking down upon him.

"The leg must come off, man." The doctor said. "Drink the whiskey and bite on this... give me a nod when you're ready."

Edward thought about it as he downed the draught and chose to live another day. "Ay Doc, when yer ready."

He clenched his teeth on the offered piece of wood, losing consciousness as the first cuts were made.

A few months later in September 1781, Edward sat astride a horse on his way to New York City and what was left of the British Army there. His leg hurt as it chafed against the saddle, but he'd padded it with a blanket wrapped and tied around the stump which gave him some relief.

He made his way north alone until he met Doc Jackson walking the same direction from Yorktown. Edward learned from him that Lt. General Cornwallis had surrendered and they made their way safely to New York.

In early 1782 Edward and Robert secured ship's passage to Scotland and home.

Upon arrival, Edward rested two nights in Greenock; the ship's conditions had been rough, but even the daily rice ration, a main staple onboard, was preferable to the meager nutrition he'd had before leaving America.

He obtained a horse and set out to Wodegate as soon as he could. It'd been nearly seven years since he left his homeland and he stopped to gaze over the estate's green slopes and gave thanks to God for the sight.

The familiar surroundings were a gentle sight after war's ravages and the terrible sights he'd witnessed. Many were the nights he'd gone to his blankets with stomach empty and no food for the morning. He'd never forget the southland of America, full of biting insects, venomous snakes and rebels who hid in its dense foliage, swamps and woods. He put the thoughts behind as his leg's throbbing reminded him promised rest lay ahead and he urged the tired horse onward.

The steps of the castle lay cluttered with trash and debris when he arrived; the surrounding gardens were unkempt, their weeds reaching above brick pathways. He turned to look over the farm fields, but they laid fallow with fences in disrepair. After tying off the horse he made his way with a make-shift crutch up the front steps to the entrance he knew so well; the doors stood bolted and he lifted both the lion's head rings to bang against them, but no one came.

He remounted and kept a strong hand on his weary horse as it snorted then reared, not in favor of carrying him further. Edward calmed him and rode to the back of the castle.

There, the familiar face of a kitchen maid broke into a smile; older now than when he'd left, she came to take hold of his horse.

"Sir, it's wunnersome to see ye; we feart ye were killt in the Americas."

"Aye, they tried, but only teuk my leg." He acted the brave one, but the stump was hurting bad.

"Whit hae happent here lass; whaur's Arden and whit for the land leas withoot keepin?"

"Ay Sir, tis sorry A'm ta say they let go Arden efter ye left and Master Willum hae teuken haud of the estate, he and his lads."

At that moment the kitchen door opened and two of Edward's nephews strutted out onto the landing. They ordered, "Gi back ta yer chores" and the kitchen maid scurried back inside. They looked at Edward with sneering smiles. "Well, leuk wha's comin aboot, thinkin ye goin ta take over the traces agin, do ye?"

"A'm your Uncle Edward, dae ye hae mynd o' me? Ye must be Chauncey and you, Willum. Whaur's yer father, A'd have a word wi himsel."

"He's inside but sent us ta hae a word wi ye. He awns the estate now, not ye who should be deid as thocht;

shame yer not, but too late noo; the courts awairded the estate legal to im. So gi on your way sir, yer no walcome and don't be returnin or we'll shaw ye how we haundle yer kine."

They started down the steps toward him and Edward drew his sword from his belt. "Haud on, A'm ill-pleased tae draw a swuird tawart faimley; A suggest ye get yer father doon here." They stopped at the sight of the highlander sword and stepped back.

"Jest calm down man." Chauncey said and ordered his brother. "Go fer father."

Soon William made his appearance outside the door, but wouldn't come to Edward. "Whit're ye doin here Edward; be ye a ghost?"

"Nay, no ghost Willum, but maybe ye whist it so?" Edward said.

"We thochtit efter seven years man." William bore the same sneer as his sons. "Ye war reckoned deid by the Court whan A teuk Wodegate."

"Whit aboot my Will sent to ye whan A left? And whit of Arden?"

"A gatna Will." William said. "An Arden is awa-gaun; drunkart he be and uissless."

"Yer leein; pack yer misbehauden rag-fowk an depairt this place. A'm alive which ye'll soon diskiver if ye dinna obey." Edward raised his sword; the sneer faded from William's face.

The boys came by their father, but he put his arms out to prevent their attack. "A suggest ye gi ower and leave afore A lowsen my lads." He peered through rheumy eyes. "Yer missin a leg, choose yer battles; it's likely unwice ta noo lat it be, brother. Hate ta see ye comin frae the War ta lose yer life hereaboots."

Edward knew he was right and turned his horse. "Whit's fur ye'll no go by ye Willum... this isna over yet."

William's face turned paler and his two young whelps giggled like lasses as Edward rode away.

'The divil haes takken ma haudin.' Edward thought. 'Be it ta lest thing, t'wil be put right afore I dee.'

CHAPTER Twelve - Returning

"Agnes!" Shelley stepped forward to hug the old housekeeper as she peered out the doorway. At that moment, Jakke barked in his big dog voice from somewhere behind her.

"Oh Jakke, don't you remember me?" Shelley called to him. The dog sidled up to her and placed his large muzzle in her hand. The light of recognition came too soon for her as he rested his front paws on her shoulders to place several sloppy kisses on her face.

Nicholas pulled him away and kept a steady hand on his collar until the dog calmed. "Nothing's changed here." He said with a grin.

"Oh Mr. Wodehouse, it's good to see ya and how are ya." Agnes welcomed him, her face wreathed in smiles. "My, what a surprise; I niver expected either one of ya again and that's the truth. Come in, come." She urged them across the threshold and shut the big door. "And what brings ya this way?"

"Shelley's here from America for a few days and we wanted to visit the estate again." Nicholas said. "You're looking good Agnes." She blushed at his remark.

He decided to ask what was on his mind. "Tell me... what's the status of the estate at this point; does Mr. Bailey visit much?"

"Ach, that one." Agnes waved her hand as if shooing off an annoying fly. "Mr. Bailey comes ta walk the grounds and castle every couple of weeks. After he makes sure repairs are bein kept up, he gets in his car and returns ta Glasgow; hard ta understand im."

"Is he treating you well?" Shelley said.

"Oh ay, I stay here now in a nice room behind the kitchen and have the whole place ta m'self. He needed someone ta stay on the property and keep an eye out for any shenanigans. We have cell phone service, can you imagine?"

"Welcome to the twenty-first century, Agnes!" Nicholas said. "Is there someone to keep the grounds and care for the horses?"

"Annie and the Black get good care; my grandson Edmund comes once-a-week ta exercise them and muck out the stalls. He's good with a lawnmower and trimmer, too. Mr. Bailey keeps him on retainer for weekends while he finishes secondary school. Come, I'll fix you something ta eat. Did ye juist get in, Ms. Shelley?"

They followed her across the great hall and through the passageway into the kitchen. "We have somethin else since ye left; a water-closet lies behind that door." Agnes pointed with pride.

"I'm first." Shelley joked.

Nicholas sat at the table while Agnes readied some sandwiches. "How have you been? You and Ilsa remained in my thoughts over the years; you both did a fine job, and I didn't say goodbye or thank you."

"Ach, no need for thanks, I'twas our pleasure sir. Those were rough days after ye left. Mr. Bailey finally came from Glasgow for several weeks to oversee repairs ta the roof and have the plumbing installed. He was true fair with Ilsa and me, gave us both a small raise he did. He offered me the permanent job livin on the estate and said with my experience, I'd know when somethin was amiss. Since my husband had passed, I accepted and let my cottage to our daughter and Edmund.

"It's quiet up here after the village, but we have television now and the place is less dismal. No 'drip-drip-drip' when it rains either; the new roof is solid and keeps us nice and dry. Here I'm going on and on, you'll be sorry ye asked. Ah, here she is; come and sit with us, Miss."

"This is lovely, thank- you Agnes. You don't know how many times I've remembered that delicious pie you and Ilsa made while I was here."

"The apple tree still bears fruit as sweet ever." Agnes said. "Ilsa's married to a nice young man. They have a boy and another wee bairn on the way in a few weeks."

"Oh, that's wonderful; please give her our love." Shelley said as she spread a muffin with butter and raspberry preserves.

"Has Mr. Bailey discussed his plans for the estate?" Nicholas said.

"Nothing with me sir, but he is fond of the place and visits more often. From the look of it, he hates ta leave."

"Interesting." Nicholas glanced at Shelley. "When is he due again?"

"Oh, within a day or two; did ye wish ta meet with him sir?"

"Let me think on it first; in the meantime, we want to take a ride around the estate before we leave. Are the horses in good stead?"

"Ay sir, healthy and full of sass, Edmund sees to that."

"Shelley, are you game?"

A smile lit up her face. "Yes, I'd love it."

They'd both brought a change of clothes and warm jackets; the sun was high, but afternoon coolness would creep up the glen in a few hours.

In the stables, the Black skittered from Nicholas' hand as he extended it. After a preliminary sniff and snort, he calmed to let Nicholas stroke his neck and talk to him, quieting in a few minutes.

The horses were full of spirit on the trail to the river and took their riders safely to the water's edge. Nicholas dismounted and helped Shelley from the mare then handed her a pair of binoculars from his jacket pocket.

He led the way to a high rock by the river's edge and they climbed the few feet to its top. From there they could clearly scan the surrounding hills, and pointed out those that fit Edward's description. Two were intriguing, with a large, gray boulder on each of their slopes.

"We can hike to one tomorrow, provided we stay overnight." Nicholas returned their glasses to his jacket pocket. "If you want to stay back, I'll set out in the morning."

"Are you kidding, I can't miss this; which one will we choose first?"

He pointed to the slope northwest of the castle. "An old logging road leads up to reforested land there, and the boulder is a short hike from its end. The other one will be more difficult to reach; we'll go to the tree line then cut east."

It'd been a while since Shelley hiked in the mountains at home, but she was excited and felt equal to the challenge.

"Tomorrow we'll get up early, eat a good breakfast, pack lunches and get on the road by seven." Nicholas left no room for discussion.

"Ay Sir!" She saluted him and received a strange look for her efforts. Darned Scots, no sense of American humor, she thought.

Nicholas pushed through the kitchen door, holding it for Shelley. "Agnes, may we have rooms for the night?"

"Of course; yer old rooms are in good shape. Mr. Bailey won't mind yer staying, dae you think, sir?"

"No, I don't Agnes, but we'll find out if he shows."

"It'll be fine." She said. "And now I'm off to my room for a nap. Supper at six, see you both then."

The next morning Nicholas drove the all-terrain vehicle over the bumpy old access road as the sun's first rays appeared over the ben. His driving was a tad scary to Shelley, and she tightened her seat belt. This has turned him into a dare devil she thought as she watched for rocks and potholes ahead.

"You okay?" He said after she grabbed the frame to brace herself.

"Yes, I've never rode in one of these." With time, she adjusted enough to laugh whenever they bounced in their seats. "This is more fun than the bumper cars at the carnival."

Nicholas glanced at her quickly and noticed her face was flushed; very becoming he thought, but put his eyes back on the difficult terrain ahead.

They reached the end of the service road in less than an hour; the ground ahead of them was rough with small rocks, grasses, scrub pines and heather bushes. "Someone better experienced with the all-terrain might carry forward, but it's safer to hike the rest of the way and give the ecology a break; you okay with it?" He said.

"Sure." Shelley jumped out of the vehicle and put on the knapsack containing their snacks and water.

Nicholas chose a direction, and she followed him along a narrow deer path that wound several yards up the hill until it veered off to the east. With the boulder in sight, they continued to ascend through the rock-strewn hillside, blazing their own trail.

Shelley sat to rest a few moments and looked over the river which moved below them through the strath; she loved the sound of the word 'strath' since hearing it earlier from Nicholas when he described the river's valley. He sat beside her and she offered one of her snack bars.

"Are you, tired?" He asked.

"It's more uphill exercise than I've had in a while, but I'm fine. The air is wonderful, isn't it? I'm so enjoying this."

Shelley looked upward to their destination. "The boulder looks lonely by itself up there; why is the grass so green around it when everything else is brown this time of year?"

"Stones soak up and hold moisture then release it to the ground around them." Nicholas said. "I don't know much geology, but these single boulders are ancient; many date back to volcanic origin, some from glacial movement. This one may have simply fallen from a rocky crag, like that one above us." Nicholas pointed to a gray rock formation several feet up the hill. "When sheep were on the estate, they grazed these high grassy patches."

He turned to look at her. "Are you ready to walk again? Here, let me carry this for a while." He lifted the knapsack from her shoulder and put it on his.

"That's not necessary." She protested.

"I know you're strong, but I like to share the load when I can." He smiled at her and continued up the hill.

What can I say to that she thought; besides, she did feel lighter, but wouldn't admit it if he asked.

The boulder was larger than it appeared from below and towered over them. Shelley placed her hand upon its coolness and its rough surface hinted of past centuries. They circled the stone together knowing the thistle carved long ago might be weathered away, but they remained optimistic. But indeed, after a thorough search, there was no sign one had existed.

"It's alright." Shelley attempted to comfort the sullen Nicholas. "We've eliminated one of two choices; tomorrow we'll tackle the other."

"And what if it's unmarked, too?" He said as they started back.

"We'll call Jessica and visit her next." Shelley was determined they'd not be beaten.

They made a fresh start in the morning for the boulder east of Wodegate. After bringing the all-terrain through to the tree line, they hiked the rest of the way.

Unlike yesterday's boulder, its south side was lightly covered by white lichens and they looked for indentations then used a wire brush sparingly to expose the stone. Still, their efforts yielded no proof of a thistle mark and in Nicholas' mind it represented a dead-end. He remained silent during their return; Shelley knew nothing she might say would make him feel better.

Agnes greeted them as they came through the kitchen door. "Well, back from the woods they come. Will ye have tea now before ye leave for Glasgow?"

"I'd love it, thank-you; give me ten minutes." Shelley left for a hot shower and change of clothes while Nicholas stayed behind.

"There's something I want to tell you, sir." Agnes said. "Mr. Bailey called and he's planning to come up tonight."

"Did you tell him we were here?"

"No, I did not. I thought ye might want the choice of leaving before he arrived."

Nicholas hesitated a moment. "Thank you for that, but I believe we'll stay tonight and leave in the morning. To explain our being here though, I insist on paying for a three night stay for a bed and breakfast arrangement." He handed three bills to her from his wallet.

"I appreciate your reasoning sir." Agnes said.

Shelley entered and saw the transaction. "What's up?"

"Just paying Agnes for our stay; Wilson Bailey will be in tonight and I don't want him to think we're taking advantage of him. It's a good idea to see him while we're here; this stand-off has lasted long enough."

Shelley noticed a smile on his face and tried to understand what he was up to then remembered Edward's words.

"Why yes, it's a perfect time to get reacquainted." She said.

Agnes knew something was afoot, but ignored it. "Let's have our tea before it chills, shall we?" She'd always thought Shelley was a perfect match for her former, moody boss and seeing them together again confirmed it.

CHAPTER Thirteen – Wilson Bailey

Wilson Bailey, of Bailey & Company Steel, Ltd. closed his laptop with a bang and swiveled his executive chair around to glare out the window.

He'd chosen this office for its panorama of his mill across the tarmac where the high wide door into the building afforded him a view of his investment. He often watched as the molten steel poured into the casting machine on its forty-five minute schedule. His favorite view was during rainfall when the sky was dark and the steel's color showed golden hot like dragon's breathe from a cave.

It was a thrill that once signified his life's goals, but with his wife's exodus last year and subsequent divorce, much feeling in his life had drained from him. More often in these times, rare memories of his mother and his austere young life flickered across his mind.

His father, a dock worker in Glasgow, had worked hard to keep them housed and fed, but it was never enough. Mum left when Wilson was ten and he didn't blame her. Winters were worst in their little flat when heat was a luxury and a bucket of coal a rarity. The trait of patience in adversity was not his father's and after she left he chose to take it out on his children.

It was ironic his dad never accepted help from Grandfather Charles; though offered many times, his reply was always the same, 'too proud' and 'we'll survive'. Under his father's unknowing influence, Wilson made his mind up early on how he'd live life and raise his own children someday, vowing never to be proud at the expense of his family. Little did he know there would be no children in his life on whom to bestow his early-learned lessons.

He'd graduated secondary school against the odds and pushed to university for a graduate in business by the time Grandfather died. His own father was already dead from an earlier dockside shipping container accident. Wilson knew what to do with his grandfather's mill and other assets; though times were rough for Scotland's steel industry, he believed it worth renovating the mill in readiness for the industry's return.

He thought about his Grandfather Charles as he continued to stare out his office window. Charles was an eccentric and lived in a dilapidated mansion outside Glasgow when he died; the duty fell to Wilson to clean out the house and make decisions on its disposal.

The old man had been an avid collector and genealogist for the Bailey family line; Wilson knew nothing of his ancestors and assumed they'd always been a lower-class lot. After hired men packed up grandfather's files and books, Wilson stored them at his home in the attic; 'plenty of time after retirement to explore these' he told himself.

What did intrigue him at the time was the Leasehold document dated 1925 he found among grandfather's papers. It was for an old estate named Wodegate and at first, he'd put it aside thinking, how valuable could it be when no one has lived there for decades? He envisioned the castle, a leaky, broken piece of history, and deemed it typical of many that sat empty across the landscape of Scotland, financially unsupported, and unloved.

Several years later the steel industry remained unchanged and growing wary of his finances, Wilson revisited the document then decided to take a ride to the property to explore its assets.

Castles were for the privileged few and the Queen he'd thought, not the Baileys; then Wodegate loomed out of the forest ahead of him, a leftover from medieval days with two towers, a drained moat and a dungeon in the basement. He felt a twinge of excitement as he walked part of the grounds then entered the building. There were many leaks in the roofs, but otherwise, it was in surprising good repair for its age.

He confessed to none but himself that he wondered what it would be like to live there. Could it be a symbol of his place in the world, timeless as years passed? But with further thought, he clung to the dream his grandfather endowed him, knowing the castle required the same money as the mill did to breathe life again. His decision made, he inserted the old iron key to the doors and took the document to his solicitor for review.

A month later, his hopes were high when he received the solicitor's call; he needed to sell the estate and use the resultant funds to buoy up his depressed steel plate business until National recovery arrived.

"A last member of the William Wodehause line died in 1924 and your grandfather Charles filed for possession as descendant of one John Benjamin Bailey." The solicitor stopped to rummage through the stack of papers in front of him.

"Court found for Charles, but granted him Leasehold status only; apparently there was questionable doubt in the legalities between an Edward and William Wodehause over the original transfer of the property."

"What do you mean; can funds be extracted or not?" Wilson said.

"You have rental rights, for such as farming and timber. Court action by surviving Wodehouse descendants with sound evidence could reverse the Leasehold and award the estate to its true heir." The solicitor looked at him and said. "Any monies you invest might be irrevocable."

Wilson returned home emotionally drained at the solicitor's news and threw the document into a drawer. Far too busy to pay attention to the needs of Wodegate, he did acknowledge the place needed a controlled investment for future roof repairs; he posted an estate manager position before he returned to the mill's affairs.

He recalled his surprise when a Nicholas Wodehouse contacted him a week after the posting. Wilson assumed he was a distant relation to the seventeenth century family, but thought little of it. In a country overrun with descendants of this and that position, most had come away from their lofty beginnings to earn money and live as 'regular folk'. Besides, this educated young man might prove to be an asset to him someday.

At the time, he'd put away any nonsense he'd considered for making Wodegate profitable; steel was what his family came from and he'd see it rally again and be ready for it.

Now at sixty-five with perfect hindsight, he stared out the window at the remains of his lofty aspiration and realized his dreams had been... just dreams.

CHAPTER Fourteen - Truths

The great door of the castle opened and slammed against the brusque wind outside. Nicholas and Shelley turned from the crackling hearth in the great hall and stood, but Wilson stayed on the landing a moment while he focused on and tried to place his unexpected guests.

Nicholas came first with his hand extended. "Wilson; Nicholas Wodehouse here, it's been a while."

Wilson recognized him then and shook his hand. "Yes, it's been what, five... six years; what are you doing here?"

"I wanted to show a good friend the Scotland you and I both know through Wodegate, I hope you don't mind. We've prepaid Agnes for a three night's bed and breakfast stay and have been hiking in the hills today." Before Wilson could reply, Nicholas continued. "Forgive me; this is Shelley Lindquist from Atlanta, Georgia."

She came forward to shake his hand and gave him her best southern smile. "Mr. Bailey; how nice to meet you. Agnes has been telling us of the wonderful repairs you've made to the castle. What a showpiece, I can't wait to tell my friends, they'll no doubt want to stay here, too. Georgia is a big outdoor-sports State and people would travel here for the deer and the river fishing alone."

Wilson was at a loss for words but did manage a half-smile at Shelley's breathless greeting. Nicholas seized the moment to further persuade him. "Won't you sit for a while with us? We'd love to hear about your steel business."

With the mention of his favorite subject, Wilson Bailey recovered. "Well... yes, I guess I could visit for a while. I'm not used to finding anyone here but Agnes; it's nice to have company for the evening." He hung his coat in the entry closet just as Agnes came from the kitchen.

"Good evening sir and how was your trip?" She said.

"I made good time, but left without dinner; any leftovers for a wee bite?" He had an afterthought. "And bring the scotch, too."

They returned to the fireside and Wilson stood in front of its warmth. "So you're from the States, Ms. Lindquist."

"Yes, I live with my two boys and mother outside of Atlanta."

"I've never been there, but I'd like to visit someday. My business doesn't allow for much travel so even the drive up here has become a pleasant break for me." Wilson looked at Nicholas and took a seat nearby. "What have you been doing since you left?"

Nicholas chose his words carefully. "I returned to my law practice in Aberdeen for a year, but decided to move back to Glasgow."

"You still have family here then?" Wilson said.

"No; both my parents have passed. And what of you; your wife is in good health?"

"She is... and lives in the States, as a matter of fact... New York; we've divorced."

"Sorry to hear that, Wilson."

"What's your impression of Wodegate?" Wilson changed the subject. "It's different since you were last here."

"Why yes, glad you've repaired the roofs and Agnes approves of the updated plumbing." Nicholas said.

Wilson laughed at his reference to Agnes. "Yes, it was an answer to prayer in her mind. Good old gal that one; not afraid of hard work and cheerful. That's why I wanted to reward her with a permanent position and quarters here."

Nicholas noticed a pleasant change in him. Years ago, his strictly business attitude and cold approach discouraged conversation or friendship; divorce and advancing age must have changed him.

Agnes brought Wilson a hot beef sandwich, a bottle of soda and the local scotch.

"Ah, thank you, Agnes." Wilson held up the bottle. "Nicholas, Shelley?" Both nodded. "Single malt made locally; see what you think." Both Shelley and Nicholas received a generous draught in straight-side whiskey tumblers and Wilson made a toast; "To a renewed acquaintance and a lovely new one."

Shelley took a light sip from her glass; her drinking experience was zero and scotch had a reputation. A surprising burn down her throat ended with heat that spread over her face.

Nicholas and Wilson were smiling as she waited for the redness on her face to subside. "Okay guys," Shelley said, "I guess you can see I'm no good at this."

They both laughed. "Now give it a chance, lass." Wilson said. "It's an acquired taste, you either like it or you don't - no matter."

"Perhaps some soda?" Nicholas said and drank a quarter of her glass then filled it back up with soda and ice.

"Thank you." Shelley accepted the revision with a skeptical look before sampling it.

"Better?" Wilson asked.

"Yes, much."

"Good. Now Nicholas, you say you've moved to Glasgow; I imagine you see changes there since you left."

"Yes, I was surprised to see the old steel mills hadn't reopened. Forgive my ignorance, but has there been any progress toward that?"

Wilson put his glass on a nearby table. "There are larger corporations rumored to be in the offing, but it hasn't happened yet."

"And what of your mill, Wilson?" Shelley said.

"Ah, a fair question, lass, but one not easily answered at this point, you see I'm caught in a dilemma. My grandfather never accomplished his dream of success and I vowed to alter that, out of respect for him. But given the continuing dormancy in Scotland's steel industry… let's say I've done my best and leave it at that. I'm not as young as I once was." He said and turned to Nicholas.

"So you're here until tomorrow morning? Why not stay another day and we'll get ourselves to the river for some fishing? It's end of salmon season, but they'll be around for a couple of weeks yet. I promised Agnes on my last visit to get one in the freezer." Wilson said.

Nicholas looked at Shelley. "Can we stay? I haven't been fishing since I was a lad."

"If you wish." She said.

"Wonderful." Wilson said. "I'll let Agnes know and we'll get an early start, say eight a.m.? Now I bid you both good night, it's been a long day." He took his sandwich and retired upstairs.

Shelley turned to Nicholas. "He's an interesting man and reminds me of you in a way; his heritage has shaped his life."

"There was a time I wouldn't be compared to Wilson, but years change us all and it's obvious we've both mellowed." Nicholas drained the last of his scotch.

"Shall we go upstairs? I have an early date with a fish tomorrow, but you can sleep late."

"I may do that." Shelley said.

The next morning, Agnes laid a hearty breakfast on the table for the men and made sure they had a knapsack full of snacks, water and a thermos of coffee to take along. They left eager to reach the river before the mists lifted.

Shelley slept in until nine a.m. and was happy to see the sunshine at the window proving the men had good weather.

After oatmeal and toast, she visited the library and was happy to see the books still on their shelves. She'd feared Wilson planned to sell them and their presence was comforting.

With flashlight in hand, she took advantage of her time alone and explored the higher bookshelves. By ten-thirty, she'd covered half of the room's upper shelves; plenty of classic literature, but none with info on the castle. Concentrating on the ladder's rungs as she climbed down, she glanced at a book on the shelf behind the ladder; it was entitled, History of The Wodegate

Estate. She moved the ladder and pulled the heavy book off the shelf to carry down to the desk.

It was a beautiful, well-preserved edition, leather bound with gilded pages and she caught her breath as she read its authors; 'Written by Brych Edward Wodehause and Christian Edward Wodehause, published in 1852'. The heavy paper was excellent quality, the print, early handset type. Surely there's something in here to help us she thought, if Edward's story carried to Brych, there'll be mention of it and she brought the volume back to her room to examine.

She tried to remain calm and objective, but it was hard not to place all hope in the tome. The morning sped by until she realized she was hungry and left her work to get lunch.

The men entered the kitchen triumphant, their faces shining as she rounded the kitchen's doorway. Nicholas held a large salmon up to show her.

"A thirty pounder, I'd say." Wilson announced with pride.

"He caught it." Nicholas said.

"Ah, but ya made a valiant effort and lost one just this size." Wilson added. "Now let's help Agnes get the monster cleaned. I say we take a few steaks off for dinner tonight before we put the rest inta the freezer, eh?"

Shelley spoke first, "We must return today, I have a pre-scheduled visit with an old friend while I'm here and don't wish to disappoint her."

Nicholas was a bit confused by her answer, but played along. "Yes, I wish we could, but we've already stayed a day over Shelley's plans for this visit."

"In that case, why don't I send two steaks home with ya in a cooler? You kin cook them up yourselves. Agnes, can you remember to do that, please?" Wilson said.

"Yes sir, it'd be my pleasure."

Nicholas went off with Wilson to help clean the fish and Shelley returned to her room on the premise of packing. She opened the book again, but with more than a thousand pages, their time at Wodegate wouldn't be enough.

Struggling with her conscience, she thought of taking the book without Wilson's permission, but her heart said 'no'. The reason was right and Nicholas should have the evidence he searched for, but sending bad Karma around could only muddy his chances. She left to secure a private word with him, out of earshot of Wilson and found both men back in the kitchen discussing the finer points of fly-fishing.

"Oh boy, there's a definite air of fish in here." She joked.

"Really; I can't smell it." Nicholas said. "I guess that's my cue to hit the showers. Wilson... thanks for the fishing this morning, I enjoyed it."

"Come up again lad; there's trout in the river we haven't caught yet."

In the hallway upstairs, Shelley motioned to Nicholas to come to her room; he followed and closed the door. "What's this all about?"

"You still smell." She informed him with a wrinkled nose.

"Well thank-you very much." He quipped. "Anything else?"

"Yes, I need to show you something." She led him to the book.

Nicholas read the title. "Where did you get this?"

"I found it on a high shelf in the library this morning; you've never seen it?"

"No, and I thought I'd explored most of those books. It's amazing, these are my grandfathers; have you had time to read any of it?"

"Some." Shelley said. "It's far too large to read now though; might Wilson let us 'check it out' for a few days if we asked?"

"I don't know." He sat on the fireplace bench. "We risk revealing we have ulterior motives for being here and it may destroy any trust he's placed in me."

"But he'd understand your interest in the book; you're related to the Wodehause family, surely he recognizes that."

"One might think so." Nicholas stayed silent while he tried to reach a decision. In a few minutes he was on his feet.

"It's time to make my case and I'd rather it were here than in a court. Besides, I've decided the most important part is to restore my grandfather's name to the estate's records. If Wilson knows that's my goal, maybe he'll be more willing to work with me. We could come to a fair contract and attempt to make the place pay for itself again."

"Love the sound of that." Shelley said. "Don't forget, you and Wilson are distant cousins; you might mention it up front."

"It could be to my benefit. I'm going to clean up now and I'll come back to carry the book downstairs. Thank-you Shelley for your help in this, I mean it." He hugged her then, not something he'd planned to do. She accepted the hug, not something she'd imagined.

Wilson sat in the library mulling over his business and Wodegate; two subjects once clear in his mind, but now opposed to each other. He admitted his grandfather's steel mill had become a burden, his zeal and high hopes for its success were gone. The questions as yet unanswered; should he sell the mill and put the money into the estate; or lease the estate's grounds to grazing or, the least favorite of his choices, lease to a high dollar building development?

Erasing history with new buildings and golf courses wasn't what he wanted for Wodegate; it made him realize he didn't look at it as 'just business' anymore. He had a need to be connected to something that mattered and Wodegate filled that need.

Nicholas and Shelley approached from the hallway and he noticed the large book Nicholas carried. "I see you've been doing light reading."

Nicholas smiled and placed the book in front of him. "Shelley found this here in the library while we were fishing and thought it might have genealogy facts for the Wodehause line."

"Did you find it helpful?" Wilson said.

They'd both taken seats in front of his desk. "We don't have enough time here to find out." Shelley said.

Nicholas dove in. "I'd like to discuss something with you, Wilson."

"Of course, I'm not due back in Glasgow until tomorrow, what is it?" Wilson said.

"First, you may or may not know…" Nicholas took a breath. "You and I are related."

Wilson leaned forward, "What do you mean 'related'; how?"

"Through my 8th removed grandmother, Anne Bailey Wodehause. Her brother was your several times removed grandfather and we are distant cousins; do you want to see the genealogy chart?"

"It would help me to understand." Wilson said. The name Anne Bailey was familiar, but he couldn't recall where he'd heard it.

Nicholas retrieved a copy of the chart he'd left in the book of Shakespeare and spread it on the desk. "Here's my grandmother Anne Bailey Wodehause in the 17th century, her son Edward and his brother William."

Wilson straightened. "My grandfather kept the family records and may have known this. When he died, I stored everything in the attic and take no pride in saying I haven't examined them yet."

"There's more to this story." Nicholas said. "The estate's loss began with my 7th removed grandfather, Edward, who left to fight in the seven year war."

"Quite a distinction." Wilson said.

"Nicholas and Anne rebuilt this castle and it passed to Edward as the eldest. His brother William claimed Wodegate for his own while Edward was at war. We believe Edward did return, but William refused to restore the property to him or to his son Brych. The estate stayed in William's line until the last heir died in 1924." Nicholas finished.

The year clicked in Wilson's mind; he knew his grandfather claimed the Leasehold in 1925 and now it made sense; his solicitor had mentioned Anne Bailey's name and foretold the last heir to Wodegate might appear.

For a while he couldn't speak. How typical he thought; Nicholas came here under false pretense to win me over then take what's his. "Have you come to take Wodegate from me then?"

Nicholas' answer was surprising. "No, I haven't."

"Then what?" Wilson demanded, knowing they must want the estate, why else were they here?

"I believe Wodegate means something to both of us." Nicholas said. "Because of my heritage, I have a duty to my grandfather to right the wrong that William perpetrated."

Wilson stood. "Then ya do plan ta drag me inta court."

"No, it's not what I want." Nicholas attempted to reassure him. "You have the Leasehold received legally by your grandfather. I want you to know up front, I consider you family as of this weekend. Whether you believe me is your decision, but I hope through our joint effort, we'll be able to preserve this Wodehause ancestral home. I'm asking for correction of the historical record only and Edward's name acknowledged as the legal owner of Wodegate with his return from the war."

"Still, where does that leave me?" Wilson said. "If changed through the courts, the Leasehold may dissolve." He put his hands on the desk. "I've come to admire this ancient home; it's the bright spot in my life…" He faced Nicholas. "I won't give it up easily." His voice was strong, his intent solid.

"Then don't." Shelley spoke. "Listen to Nicholas, hear his ideas and share yours with him. Together you two can work out a plan to save Wodegate as a family heritage that belongs to each of you. Wilson, you have a mind for business and Nicholas practices law. Two people with those talents in a joint venture could be outstanding in their accomplishments. Neither of you had much family life; this is your chance to build something for future generations."

Both men sat again, her words hanging between them. Time slowed and Shelley wasn't sure either of them could reach the conclusion she favored.

Wilson finally spoke. "Does this mean yer stayin for dinner then?" He allowed a foxy grin to spread across his face.

Nicholas reached to shake his hand, a smile upon his face as well. "Yes, I believe it does Wilson."

Shelley was ecstatic and went to each one to give them a hug. "Bravo—well done." She said and noticed that Nicholas kept her in his arms a few seconds longer than she intended.

CHAPTER Fifteen – Trails

Nicholas and Shelley left Wilson in good spirits the next morning. Rather than return to Glasgow, they saved hours by leaving Wodegate to see Jessica in Inverness.

It was a good decision to bring the truth to Wilson. They'd stayed up late the night before to share ideas and planned a joint meeting in Glasgow with their attorneys to draft up an agreement. The pressure to save the estate was off and it cleared the way to continue their search on Edward's behalf.

Wilson gave the book to Nicholas to keep as long as they needed it. "Bring it back when you're finished." He said.

Shelley used the road time to study more of the book. Though Brych likely helped with the early rough drafts, his son Christian must have worked for years after his father's death in 1830 to finish the book. She could only imagine the depth of stories shared between father and son.

"Find anything interesting?" Nicholas said as they neared Inverness.

"Everything in this book is fascinating, but nothing yet on Edward and William's split." Shelley said. "There's so much information, it'll take weeks to get through it."

"We're near Jessica's; are you showing the book to her?"

"Yes, but I won't leave it; it may be the only one of its kind."

Jessica Davies lived in a modest two-story cottage just outside Inverness. They walked through a lovely flower garden in the front yard to ring the bell and Jessica flung the door open to greet them.

"Nicholas and Shelley! I'd know you anywhere from Janet's description. Welcome."

Her curly brown hair bounced as she led them into her lounge- turned - office at the back of the house; a large window faced a flourishing vegetable garden.

"Are you the gardener?" Shelley said.

"Oh I wish." Jessica said. "My husband's hobby; doesn't he do a beautiful job? I stay busy with my family history clients and can't give gardening the time it deserves. Besides, see this thumb; its brown isn't it?" They laughed at her self-effacing humor. "Please, sit here. How long do we have? There's a lot of research to bring you up to date on."

"We have hours to spare before returning to Glasgow; we've come from Wodegate and a visit with Wilson Bailey." Nicholas said.

Jessica sat back in her chair. "I'm surprised; may I ask what about?"

"Nicholas and Wilson laid the groundwork on a joint venture for Wodegate Estate." Shelley said.

"Yes, but Shelley was instrumental as a neutral party." Nicholas said. "Wilson and I realize now we're of the same family; we both love Wodegate, so why not join forces to save it."

"That's wonderful and it takes care of one item on my list; I wasn't sure you were aware of the Bailey connection. So on to the best news." Jessica reached for her notes. "Everything else is just detail for your genealogy records.

"I've found one of Arden Ross's descendants; Catherine Ross-Ramsey lives in Glasgow and is the researcher for her family's lineage."

"That's wonderful news. How did you find her?" Shelley said.

Jessica opened a folder. "By fluke as it turns out; lots of Ross families in Scotland and little time to find the right one. So, I began calling those in the Glasgow area and asking if they had an Arden Ross, circa 17th century, in their lineage.

"Catharine not only knew the name, but opened with her museum story. Her mother and father left two old and well preserved documents she didn't know what to do with so she turned them over to a local museum for care. Here's the address and the curator's phone; since you live there, Nicholas, might you go the rest of the way with him and get certified copies?"

"Absolutely; could one of these be Edward's Will?" Nicholas said.

"One was written in Gaelic and she hasn't followed up on it yet. If the museum hasn't already done so, you'll need an interpreter to translate." Jessica said and went on to her next note.

"Janet also asked me to research ship's logs for 1780-1781 because Shelley came across the English surgeon, Robert Jackson, who made a name for himself in both British and Colonial camps during the War.

"Shelley, you wondered if he'd taken care of Nicholas' grandfather when he lost his leg. I was unable to find record of that, but did find Edward's regiment and his injury date." Jessica pulled out a document copy.

"Dr. Jackson turned up as he returned to Scotland via Greenock in 1782; take a look at the names on this ship's passenger list." She handed the paper to them and wore a mysterious smile.

Fifty or more names of men and women who'd arrived from the Port of New York were written down the page. "Oh my; look at this!" Shelley pointed to the bottom of the page.

Nicholas couldn't believe his eyes; 'Edward Wodehause, age 51, citizen of Scotland, Military, 71 Queens Regiment' the entry read. "He came back on the same ship as his physician...this shows he came back in 1782 and may be enough to prove Edward survived."

"It's a step in the right direction." Jessica said. "The problem is that ship's logs were kept by crew members with next to no education, and notorious for misspellings and errors. The Court could demand additional evidence to prove this actually is Edward."

"So, this'll be our first piece and we'll add to it." Shelley said. "We'll continue until we find more; perhaps the museum documents will help."

Nicholas looked at her with appreciation. "Shelley keeps me encouraged, if she's still enthused, so am I."

"Good." Jessica said. "You know your mother described you two perfectly, Shelley."

"Oh? What did she say?"

"Nicholas will be the one discouraged and Shelley, the eternal optimist." Janet said.

"I guess that's correct." Shelley stole a sideways glance at him then looked down at the book they'd brought.

"We brought a book I found at Wodegate to show you." The weighty tome came out of the canvas bag, with help from Nicholas and he placed it in front of Janet. "It's heavy, be careful." He cautioned.

Jessica read the title. "... and look at the authors." She said. "This is quite the find, have you read any of it yet?"

"A few pages," Shelley said, "Wilson told us to keep it until we're finished."

"I'd like to copy the face page, if you don't mind, and see if it exists anywhere else." Jessica said. "Any other questions I can help you with today?"

"Have you made any progress in finding grandfather's death certificate?" Nicholas said.

"The Church of Scotland's records show nothing regarding his burial." Jessica said.

Shelley stole a look at Nicholas. "We know why there's no record, but don't ask how. Edward is buried on a hill overlooking Wodegate Estate and we've spent the last two days hiking hills with no success finding it."

"Did you summon Edward while you were there?" Jessica asked.

"You know?" Nicholas said.

"Janet shared your secret after I asked how she knew all the things she did."

"And yet you're treating us like credible human beings." Shelley said. "I'm amazed at your trust."

Jessica laughed at her. "I've never seen a departed visitor, but when it comes to the strange and unusual, I've read many such descriptions in my research work. In almost every family, stories get passed along; some people say they communicate with loved ones' thoughts from beyond, others say they've seen the person.

"Edward sounds like a very strong man in life and apparently has... permission, shall we say, to finish his unfinished business; who am I to say it's impossible?"

"Edward wasn't present when we searched." Nicholas said. "The thought didn't cross my mind since he's never been shy in reaching me when he felt it necessary."

"Then I suggest you pay a visit to the museum next." Jessica said. "If that doesn't give you something useful, a visit with Edward should be your next step. I'm happy you sorted things out with Wilson at the estate.

"What remains now is to satisfy Edward's wishes and that may not be easy. Things far in the past are better left to stand as history, but there's no reason you can't tell the corrected version and consign it to posterity yourself."

Nicholas thought out loud as they drove back to Glasgow. "Jess was right you know. We need to decide how best to correct the wrong for Edward; her idea on writing the facts from this generation is something I'm confident Wilson will support, once we set the terms of our joint venture."

"I agree." Shelley said. "Right now, I want something to eat, a hot shower, and rest. Tomorrow we'll call the museum curator and arrange a visit."

The sky opened overnight and the rain continued in the morning as they set out for the museum. Nicholas brought the car to the apartment's entry and Shelley ran across the sidewalk to jump in with the folded umbrella and shut the door. "Whew! Now I know what they mean by 'normal precipitation' in Glasgow."

"There's always a towel on the backseat this time of year." Nicholas said.

"You are a smart man." She reached into the back seat to retrieve it.

As museums go, it was of modest size tucked into an old street in historic Glasgow; the building dated back to the 1700's. Run by volunteers, it closed in September for the winter, but with a word from Mrs. Ross-Ramsey, the curator agreed to meet on-site and discuss the donated papers.

"These are what Mrs. Ramsey brought to us." He said. After giving them both a pair of cotton gloves, he laid the two documents out for perusal and explained their history.

"This is a register page from a popular Inn that sat in the docks area of Greenock; all of these signatures were entered during August, 1782. "

"But why would Arden Ross preserve this?" Shelley asked.

"There's no way of knowing." He said. "Both he and his descendants took pains to preserve and pass them along. They were layered in cotton paper and put into a leather case, passed down to Mrs. Ramsey's parents by a distant uncle."

Nicholas was reading the register while they talked and suddenly grabbed Shelley's arm. "Read this and tell me I'm not dreaming."

The entry dated August 17th, 1782, contained a signature entered by a quill pen which spattered ink as it was written. Despite that, it read 'Edward N. Wodehause' signed in for a two day stay.

"This coincides with the date on the ship's register; he must have rested before continuing to Wodegate." Shelley said. "This is our second piece of documentation."

The curator had been silent as he watched their elation. "Congratulations on your find. Would you mind sharing the information so we can record and catalogue it with the documents?"

"No, not at all." Nicolas said. "We've searched long and hard for proof of my grandfather's return from the War."

"I'll pass the news along to Mrs. Ramsey, she'll be glad to hear her contribution helped. Have you any use for the second paper?"

Nicholas tried to read it, but it was a language foreign to him. "What is this? I can't read it."

"It's a last will and testament, a mix of Gaelic and English, typical for solicitors of that age."

"Sir, we're looking for Edward's Will." Shelley said. "Arden Ross received a copy from him before he left for the War; could this be it?"

The curator looked through the pages then pushed the document closer to them. "I have good news and bad. The Will is that of Arden Ross, but the good news, the witness's signature is by Edward N. Wodehause. Though not an expert in handwriting it certainly looks like a match to that on the Inn's register, don't you think?"

"When was this signature written?" Shelley asked. Nicholas understood the date's importance and looked to the curator.

"The date of signing was April of 1785."

Nicholas sat back in relief. The date was three years after the ship's passenger list entry and the Inn's desk register signature, proving that Edward stayed in the area and found his old friend Arden.

At first Nicholas thought it solid evidence, but the more he considered it from a solicitor's perspective, the question remained; would this satisfy a Court of Law? "These documents prove only that Edward returned from the War; it doesn't show whom he designated as Trustee until Brych reached manhood. We still need the Will; it's the only way to uncover William's deceit."

Shelley's news about their museum find was music to Janet's ears, but she was concerned the Will still eluded them and called Jessica to discuss it.

"It was good news at the Museum." Jessica said to Janet. "The problem is, I've searched the Commissary/ Sheriff's record, both in Glasgow and in Edinburgh and no Will for Edward was entered in their recorded data. I'm wondering if it was ever registered; didn't you tell me that William received a copy as well?"

"Edward said he sent it to him by messenger before he left." Janet said.

"I smell a rat, don't you?" Jessica said. "If Edward told William he was leaving the continent for America, William may have thought it the perfect time to either steal the original from the solicitor in Glasgow or pay him off for not filing it; either action would have done the trick."

"You're right, but that means the only copy available was Arden's." Janet said. "Where can we go from here?"

"I think it's time to face the fact it may never be found." Jessica said.

Nicholas opened his apartment door and Shelley entered. It was late afternoon, but already dark. She'd forgotten that in this part of the world, sun light shone only seven to eight hours, if it came at all with the rainfall.

"I think I have lack of sun complex." Shelley joked.

"I have the perfect thing." Nicholas crossed the livingroom and turned on a lamp. "How's this?"

"Oh, very funny."

"No, really; it's a full spectrum light for seasonal affective disorder. Take your coat off and come over here for a while; I swear you'll feel better."

Shelley did as instructed and took to the recliner where Nicholas adjusted the long-necked lamp to shine on her face and arms. "Now don't move. I'll get you some refreshment."

"You don't have to wait on me..." She said.

"Just shhh...let me do this." He said on his way to the kitchen.

The icemaker dropped cubes into a glass and Shelley heard. "It's too early for a drink." She said.

Nicholas reappeared carrying a large glass of something light green.

"That's not a margarita is it?" Shelley said.

"It's too early per a voice heard from the kitchen, so no, this is a 'margar' without the 'ita'; fresh limeade with lots of vitamin D for your condition, I recommend it."

"Thank-you Nicholas." She took a sip. "This is the best limeade I've ever tasted."

"Good. I'm calling for takeout, do you like Chinese, Italian, Thai, what?" He asked.

"I've never had Thai, it's spicy though, isn't it?"

"Yes, it can be, but if you want to try it, I'll get an assortment in various stages of heat." He laughed.

"I'm game." She said. "You know you don't have to do all this."

"Do what? I'm being a gracious host. It's taken me a while to get the knack, but I'm evolving."

She took another sip from her glass then leaned back to relax under the light. There might be hope for 'sir' yet she thought with a smile.

CHAPTER Sixteen - Visitor

Janet took a break from her busy morning to take a final look at the Custody form Nicholas sent for her completion. All their gathered evidence would be presented to the Court with proof of chain of custody documented and she'd send the form back to Nicholas today by email. She'd included extra lines for Edward's Will, but barring a miracle, it appeared to be lost to them for all intent and purpose.

The boys were beginning to miss their mother with the holidays so near and only one more week remained until Christmas Eve.

Janet suddenly remembered they needed a tree. That'll get them out of their blues she thought as she entered the email to Nicholas then sprang up to call the boys from their rooms.

The following morning, Nicholas took the Custody form first to the museum for the curator's signature; Jessica was last on the list and happily signed as a licensed genealogy researcher in the presence of her husband. Both wished him good luck before he left to return to Glasgow.

Calm washed over him with the form completed; the job was done. He'd used every opportunity given him and the help of others to see Wodegate and the family name restored; now it would be left to the Court.

He arrived home by evening and Shelley greeted him at the door with a strange look on her face. He tried to interpret it then looked beyond her to the livingroom and saw Wilson Bailey.

"Well, this is a surprise." He said as he put his jacket and brief case aside. "How are you Wilson?"

"Hope I'm not imposing on you both." Bailey said as he shook Nicholas' hand. "Before our solicitor meeting tomorrow, I thought I'd better show you something."

"No problem, I've just been taking care of last minute details on the estate's case." His mind raced as he thought, I shouldn't have imagined this was finished, Bailey must be changing his mind. But he couldn't read the man's face and decided Wilson had the makings of a great poker player.

"I've made an important decision and want you and Shelley to be the first to know." Wilson said.

Shelley came to sit by Nicholas and took his hand. His grip tightened for a second then relaxed. "How can we help you, Wilson?"

"I've decided to sell the Mill; it was a hard decision, but the right one. I do need your help with something else though." Wilson said.

"How so?" Nicholas asked.

"I'm asking that you include my grandfather's name in the history of Wodegate for the record. It's a bit unusual, but important to me, just as Wodegate is, what do you think?"

Nicholas considered the request reasonable. "It's a good idea; I do need to have it approved by someone else." Nicholas intentionally left Edward's name unsaid; it wasn't necessary to fill in Wilson with the unusual details.

"Fair enough and I hope your solicitor sees no problem in doing so." Wilson assumed it was Nicholas' solicitor and appeared relieved.

"This brings me to the second reason I'm here." He reached into his satchel and brought out an envelope, placing it in Nicholas' hand. "You'll be interested in that."

Nicholas carefully drew out a document written in a familiar hand. Shelley gasped when she saw a Will written in English and Gaelic as Arden's had been, with one astounding difference; this one contained Edward's name in its top margin.

"I don't know what to say. How... where did this come from?" Nicholas could barely speak.

Wilson laughed. "Remember I told you there were boxes from my grandfather Charles' research in my attic? After the decision on the mill, I decided there was no excuse for ignorance of one's family and spent the day digging through them.

"I found a large box labeled 'Wodegate' and figured it contained his research for the Leasehold claim, so I brought it downstairs to sort out, with a glass of scotch, of course."

"And there it was?" Nicholas asked incredulously.

"There it was. Apparently, a man named Arden Ross used to be caretaker at Wodegate and had the Will in his possession. In failing health a few years later, he took it to the only person he trusted to keep it safe." Wilson stopped. "My throat's dry, may I have a glass of water please?"

Shelley jumped up and soon brought a glass to him, not wanting to miss a word of the story.

"Thank you Shelley." He drank from the glass and set it on the table.

Nicholas was impatient. "So where did Arden leave the Will?"

"Charles' notes say that Arden turned it over to the Baileys. John Benjamin Bailey II, my 7th removed grandfather passed it on as part of his heritage with enough information to succeeding heirs to encourage its safekeeping. The Bailey's allegiance to Anne must have provided its continued protection through the family lineage.

"As you can see, that is an official copy in your hands, signed by the solicitor who gave it to my grandfather. Per his notes, the original was entered to the National Archives of Scotland as soon as he realized its importance."

"Wilson, I don't know how to thank you. This is a gift, more than we could hope for; we'd actually given up on it since our genealogist was unable to find it at the National Archives." Nicholas turned to Shelley. "We need to let Jess know of this so she can correct the records there. Thank-you so much Wilson, this is fantastic."

"Ach, no need for thanks; the look on your face is enough and I'm happy to have found it. Now I'll be saying good night to you two and see you at the solicitors' tomorrow." He picked up his coat and accepted a hug from Shelley before leaving. "God bless you both."

In the elevator, Wilson was lighter on his feet than he'd been in years. So this is how it feels to help someone; I could use a dose of this on a daily basis he thought.

The next day their partnership contract was drawn up by four o'clock to both Nicholas' and Wilson's satisfaction. The estate's resources would be managed jointly until both men worked out details over the next few months. Wilson and Nicholas would contribute equal financial support for the daily expenses; Wilson would support any special project cost, such as lodging upgrades for hunting or fishing guests, and receive interest on his investment plus a percent of return on profits. They shook hands outside the solicitor's office.

"Wilson, I'd like you to be present when I file the claim for the estate next week." Nicholas said. "Because of you, I've added the Will to the Chain of Custody; it signifies a new beginning for both of us and you should be present."

"It'd be an honor, lad." Wilson said.

Shelley had the table set for dinner when Nicholas arrived home at six. She'd managed to cook up a meal with things she found in the cooler; a nice vegetable soup, along with crispy bread and a tart for dessert from the bakery down the street. It was a celebration of the filing for Wodegate, but she had something to tell him after dinner and hoped he'd take it well.

"Something smells good." Nicholas said as he came in. "I'm starved."

"Good, sit and I'll bring the soup." Shelley said. "How did it go today?"

"Our claim for Wodegate is officially filed and in the court system. Wilson and I will meet after the holidays to plan the estate's return to life as it were; I owe him so much."

"He certainly saved the day." Shelley took her seat at the table. "And with the two of you working together, I assume Edward's plan to take you back to the original court date is now unnecessary?"

"Yes; it's senseless to think of starting over now that we've worked out a better way. Besides, Wilson and I are different men than we were in 2002; who knows if we would have worked it out together then?"

They finished eating and brought their coffee and the tart into the livingroom where the night lights of Glasgow created a beautiful view and the lighted bridge spanned the Clyde.

"This is so good." Shelley said, licking a remnant of cherry filling from her lips.

"You missed a little ..." He said and took his napkin to wipe the corner of her mouth.

"Sorry." Her face was turning red.

"It was kind of cute." Nicholas sipped his coffee and watched her over the rim of his cup.

"We've accomplished a lot in the last two weeks together and I'm happy for you." Shelley said. "There is something I need to tell you."

"What is it?"

"I'm missing the boys and I've decided to go home for Christmas to surprise them."

His face dropped and seeing it made her heart ache. "It's up to you and Wilson now to run the estate successfully and make it live again." She said. "Edward must be so pleased." She paused to see how he was accepting her news.

"Shelley... of course you miss them, I'm sorry for being so selfish; I should have seen it. They're lucky to have you." He stood and pulled her from the couch. "But I'll miss you terribly, you know."

"I'll miss you, too." She said, letting herself be drawn into his arms.

Upon hearing that, he kissed her once gently then again with a warm passion as she returned to him what was given.

He drew back. "It'll be difficult flying with the holidays so near; do you have tickets?"

"I leave tomorrow afternoon to Kennedy then Atlanta."

He held her close again. "Then you'd better get to sleep, we'll talk tomorrow at breakfast?"

"Yes, tomorrow." Shelley said.

Nicholas sat alone staring at the river lights for hours before finally seeking sleep, but it wasn't a good night for it. He tried to envision when he'd see her again, but until Wodegate's business was underway, he couldn't leave Scotland. It was ironic that he now had everything he'd worked for and yet, without Shelley, his life would still be lacking.

Breakfast was difficult for them both; there was so much to say, but no way to say it. They talked of this and that until they finished eating.

For some reason, Shelley's eyes grew large. "Oh my gosh; I forgot to shop for the boys and I promised." She looked to Nicholas panic-stricken.

"Don't worry." He checked the clock. "The stores are just opening and we have hours before the airport, let's go."

They spent their remaining time together sharing laughter and power shopping, managing to find several gifts and toys. After dropping them to be shipped via two-day express, they arrived at the airport with a few minutes to spare.

Both hesitated until the last minute to leave their embrace at the boarding gate.

"Email?" Shelley finally asked with a brave smile.

"Every day" He promised and they sealed it with a last kiss.

On the side of the mountain is a single ancient stone. It overlooks the strath, the green hills beyond and Wodegate castle. Edward took particular pleasure in sitting there from time to time when on leave from his 'regular duties', but this was a special day. He knew Shelley and Janet, Mark and Jason flew from Georgia last night to surprise his grandson Nicholas. He thanked God for allowing him to be present this soft summer day and kept an eye out for their arrival with lightness in his soul.

CHAPTER Seventeen - Welcome

Shelley drove with care up the long tree-lined drive; Janet and the boys were so excited they could hardly bear it.

"Over there." Mark said. "I see the river. Can we go fishing Mom?"

"I'm sure Nicholas will want to take you both there, you can even ride the mare." Shelley said.

She didn't tell them she was unsure of what she'd find at Wodegate; the trip for Nicholas received very little planning and was without his knowledge. In fact, it had taken every bit of courage she could muster to do something this daring.

Nicholas was tied to the estate for the time being and spending all his time at work on projects to build revenue. Upcoming seasonal stays required some redo of the castle's rooms including installation of independent heating units and plumbing and Nicholas was doing double duty as a helper with a licensed plumber to save money on the project. Some windows needed reglasing and chimneys were also tended to. He couldn't think of making a trip to the U.S. for at least another twelve months.

Shelley thought it a great surprise if they all came to him, but now that they were here her adventurous spirit seemed to be taking leave.

When the castle came into view, Jason was the first one to speak up. "Are there ghosts in there, Mom?" He couldn't forget the night she came home from vacation. He'd stood with Grams and Mark in the hallway listening to a deep voice with a heavy accent in their mom's room.

After that, he and Mark would occasionally sneak a look at stuff Grams left on the table in the livingroom. Mark was the one who figured out who the deep voice belonged to, but they kept it secret and figured if they were supposed to know, Grams would tell them.

Besides, it was more fun to share the secret between them; sort of like being secret agents. Now they could go further in their 'investigation' and Jason couldn't wait.

"I want to explore the towers." He said.

"Okay, but don't forget, we're at someone's home not an amusement park." Shelley said. "Always ask permission before you go anywhere inside, got it?"

Both boys caught 'the stare' through the rearview mirror. "Yes mam."

She changed her stern look into a smile. It was putting them in a candy shop and saying 'don't eat', but something a mom had to do.

"Here we are." She turned off the key and everyone piled out at the same time. "Wait." She reviewed her boys to make sure they were presentable and cautioned them as they walked to the front door. "Don't forget to be polite." Janet herded them toward the door.

Shelley saw a large plaque to the right of the doors. "What's this?" She went closer to read it and Janet followed.

"How lovely of Nicholas and Wilson to mention their friends; this is so beautiful." Janet said. "Does it mean what I hope it does?"

Shelley couldn't answer at first. "I believe so, but Nicholas didn't mention it." She quickly brushed a tear from her cheek and turned to Janet. "Let's get on with this; the boys are restless."

Shelley stood before the doors, but hesitated to use the lion's head knocker. What if Nicholas has changed she thought; he may have misgivings. A moment went by then Jason took charge.

"Mom, knock on the door already will ya?" He came past her to do it himself.

"Jason!" She said. But it was too late, Jason was enjoying the noise the iron ring created and the door was soon pulled open.

"Shelley?" Nicholas stood rooted in the doorway, his shock evident.

She wanted to disappear at that moment. It was true; his feelings had changed in the four months since they'd parted in Glasgow.

"Nicholas, I'm sorry, is this a bad time? We thought we'd surprise... "

'Surprise' was her last word before he wrapped her in his arms and kissed her, taking a long, hungry taste of her after their months apart. The boys were making faces and Janet was grinning like an idiot as she watched.

When the couple realized there was silence around them they parted, but continued to stare into each other's eyes.

Janet cleared her throat, and they turned absentmindedly toward her. "Hello Nick. Hope you have your bed and breakfast in order because we're here for several weeks."

"Well of course, Janet." He said. "This is wonderful! Hey Mark, hey Jason." The boys smiled shyly and made a dash inside.

"Boys!" Shelley said, but they'd disappeared and she looked at Nicholas. "Is that dungeon still in the basement? And another thing, the sign by the door?"

"We have all kinds of things to keep eleven-year-olds busy; I don't think we'll need the dungeon; the sign will come later. I'm just glad you're here. I missed you so much." Then he turned to Janet and gave her a hug. "Come in, it's great to see you again."

Agnes had the boys at the kitchen table with a plate of cookies and milk when they found them.

"Ah, Miss Shelley." Agnes hugged her.

"Agnes, it's so good to see you again. I'd like you to meet my mother, Janet Lindquist."

"Well now Janet, I've heard all about ye from yer girl here. We'll have ta get together for a cup later and catch up, what say ye?"

"I'd love to, Agnes." Janet said.

They soon discovered Shelley and Nicholas had left the room; Agnes winked at Janet and they went back to minding the boys.

Nicholas and Shelley walked the trail to the hill's summit, catching up on their lives since they'd said goodbye, stopping occasionally to share a kiss.

When they arrived at the top of the trail, they leaned against the boulder at the stream's edge and held each other close as the noisy water made its way to the river below.

"Ay, ye did good Nicholas and ye too lass." Edward's strong voice came to them. They looked around, but couldn't see him.

"Now can I meet mine ain guid wife who waits for me, knowin all is in order. A blissin on ye both; I'll look on ye in the edge o a time." They waited to hear more and perhaps see him, but silence told the story.

Then Nicholas noticed something unusual when a beam of sunlight fell on the boulder next to them. He bent to investigate a curious indentation in the stone.

A thistle bloom, Scotland's bonnie flower, was chiseled deep into the granite with the letters 'E. N. W.' underneath it. The mark lay on the north side of the big stone, away from the trail's path where it escaped notice.

How ironic that it was here all the time Nicholas thought; they'd searched everywhere for Edward's resting place last year and never suspected it this close to Wodegate.

"I'm glad part of him lays here." Nicholas said as he took her back into his arms. "Wodegate will always be under his gaze."

"Somehow, knowing Edward, I think it would have been so, no matter what." Shelley said. "I love that whoever visits this place will see the valley and the roofs of Wodegate as he does."

Nicholas bent to kiss her again and they left Edward go.

TO All WHO PASS HERE

Know ye Wodegate Castle was built over three hundred years ago and first restored in 1680, its land reforested by
Christian Nicholas Wodehause
and his wife
Anne Bailey Wodehause.
Edward N. Wodehause continued his father's work until 1776 when he left Scotland with the 71st Fraser's Highlanders for the seven year war. He returned in 1782 and found his brother William had falsely claimed the estate and refused to yield.
Through Edward's 7th removed grandson Nicholas Edward Wodehouse; and
Anne Bailey's 8th removed grand-nephew Wilson Hebert Bailey; and with
the help of their Friends and Family,
Wodegate Castle and Estate
is again restored to
Major Edward Nicholas Wodehause
February 15, 2017

Aye Come Ye Back

The sign at the Wodegate doors.